INTIMA

Intimate Temptations 1

Nicole Morgan

EROTIC ROMANCE

Siren Publishing, Inc.
www.SirenPublishing.com

A SIREN PUBLISHING BOOK
IMPRINT: Erotic Romance

INTIMATE PERSUASIONS

ISBN-10: 1-60601-599-0
ISBN-13: 978-1-60601-599-5

First Printing: March 2010

Cover design by Jinger Heaston

Printed in the U.S.A.

PUBLISHER
Siren Publishing, Inc.
www.SirenPublishing.com

DEDICATION

I wrote *Intimate Persuasions* because I feel it addresses an issue that many couples today don't confront—their own sexual desires. All too often, we ignore want we truly want for fear of embarrassment or rejection. This story will hopefully show you that with the right person there is nothing so taboo that two people can't share with one another.

I dedicate this book to the wonderful publishers, authors, readers and friends I have met during my writing endeavors. Without your expertise or friendly advice this may not have been possible.

INTIMATE PERSUASIONS

Intimate Temptations 1

NICOLE MORGAN

Chapter One

Ann pulled to the side of the road, cursing as she brought her car to a stop. “Damn it,” she muttered as she got out and saw the evidence of the obnoxious thump that had been plaguing her for the last few minutes. *What was she going to do now?* She glanced at her perfectly manicured hands, knowing that there was no way she was going to risk damage to them while changing a tire. She sighed because despite the manicure, she had no idea how to change a tire anyway.

Frustration overcame her and she kicked the tire. In retrospect that wasn’t the best idea, seeing as how she was wearing open toed, small-heeled sandals. Hobbling and cursing, she caught sight of a car pulling up behind her. Biting her bottom lip on the pain she stood up and looked at the man coming towards her.

“Oh great,” she whispered under her breath. The man had ‘ride me’ written all over his face. If this was going to be another one of those ‘I’ll help you if you help me’ sort of things then he could forget it.

“Well, hello there pretty lady.” He spit the toothpick out of his mouth and continued, “Need a little help, do ya?”

Be nice, maybe he’s not as sleazy as he seems. “Yes, I’m afraid I have a flat tire and I don’t know how to change it.”

He nodded smugly. "That's all right darling. I'll fix you up right good."

You have got to be kidding me. The way that he was leering at her was giving his statement all sorts of alternate meanings. "Listen, I just need help with the tire. I really don't need help with *anything* else."

Not getting the hint, he came toward her. "Oh come on darling, after I fix your tire, you can thank me properly." He grabbed her.

Ann had been ready. She'd met his type before and knew that his Neanderthal persona was merely lurking beneath the surface. She struggled against him and made her first attempt to knee him in the groin. He had been ready for her also though and swiftly moved out of the way, laughing at her attempt. Her eyes widened at the thought that he might actually be able to overpower her.

He pushed her against the side of the car and ground his hardness against her. Muttering lewd things in her ear, he attempted to grab under her shirt. Struggling against him, she gave her knee another hard and swift thrust upward. She was startled and thrown off balance as her knee was met with complete air. Where did he go?

"Leave…the…lady…alone! Got it?" A tall and muscular stranger who had dark hair peeking out from underneath a Stetson shouted to the man who was now lying on the ground.

Ann stared at him, mesmerized by the glorious sight of his back side. *Damn did he look hot!* And that cowboy hat. *Yeehaw, ride 'em cowboy.* And how tall was he? At least six and a half feet. She was interrupted from her mini fantasy as he shouted at the man again.

"I said to leave the lady alone. Did you not understand that?"

Stuttering the man shuffled to his feet. "Yeah, I'm sorry. I'll go." He got up and ran to his car.

The mysterious and sexy stranger walked to the man in three strides, "Apologize to the lady, and then get your sorry ass out of here!" He was now grabbing onto his shirt and inches from the man's face.

"S-Sorry ma'am."

"Good, now get your ass out of here!"

He waited for the man to drive away before turning to face her. Oh my, if she would have gone to a sketch artist and described her ideal man she couldn't have done a better job. He was complete perfection in the masculine form. And the cowboy hat added to her fantasy about tenfold.

"Are you all right?" He walked toward her as he asked the question.

He was talking to her right? She should say something. *Yeah, definitely. Say something, anything.*

"Ma'am?"

He was closer to her now and she was fairly certain that the temperature had risen a good twenty degrees. "I ah, I'm fine."

He gave her a half smile. "Men can be real assholes sometimes, huh?"

She laughed, she couldn't help it. He was right. Men *could* be real assholes sometimes. And how nice of him to be so astute to that fact. It was, after all, partially why she had left that jerk Larry and moved here. Oh no, she suddenly remembered. The reason she was on this god forsaken dirt road in the first place. The Roadhouse. She was going to be late for her interview.

"Can you change a flat?" She asked him abruptly.

"Yes I can. You got a spare?"

A spare? What the hell is a-- oh, a spare. "Yeah, it's in the trunk."

"All right then." He walked to the back of her car and waited for her to unlock the trunk. Not even giving her the chance, he reached in and hauled the tire out. "You got an iron, a jack?"

"Huh?"

He laughed at her, "Never mind. I'll be right back."

She watched him as he walked away. Boy did she watch him. Shouldn't it be illegal for an ass to look that good?

He came back over from his truck with two objects that looked like – oh a *tire* iron and a jack. That's what he meant.

"I really appreciate you helping me out like this."

She watched in admiration as he worked his back muscles. While he was jacking up the car he turned and answered her.

* * * *

"Sure. No problem. Maybe when we're done you can give me a little sugar." He waited for her outrage to begin. He had only been kidding. But when he looked up at her, outrage was not what he saw.

"I was only kidding," he told her, very aware of his constricting jeans. If he didn't know better he would swear she had been mentally undressing him. Did it just get hotter out here? He removed his hat from his head and wiped his brow. He got a better look at her while doing so. She was a brunette, long wavy hair, with pretty almond shaped eyes. Yeah, it was definitely hotter out here.

She didn't say anything, but merely stared at him as he continued to flex his muscles while he changed her tire.

Ten minutes later he placed her flat in the trunk of her car and headed over to his truck to place his tire iron and jack back in his tool box. He brushed off his hands and was all set to turn and maybe ask her name when she was suddenly right there in front of him.

"Okay, well you're all set." Why was she looking at him like that? Like she hadn't eaten in days and he was a buffet.

* * * *

Just do it Ann. You'll never see him again. Wasn't it one of your fantasies? A hot interlude, on a hot day, with a hot guy? What woman wouldn't want to go for it, and that cowboy hat was the final straw in what she needed to just about send her over the edge. *Oh hell, who was she kidding? She was already over the edge!* Not giving herself time to think twice she grabbed onto his snug fitting shirt and dove in for glory.

* * * *

He was startled as his hat flew off from her attack. She was devouring him, ravishing him with every swipe of her tongue. He was shocked for a moment, not sure what to do. Then like a tornado of lust it all came back to him. He slid his tongue inside her mouth and danced it all around inside, relishing in the feeling of the velvety heat of her kiss. Reaching down and around he grabbed onto her ass and lifted her to him.

He gritted his teeth at the feel of her legs wrapping around his waist. Her kisses were erotic. Had he ever been kissed so aggressively by a woman before? He didn't think so, because with every glide of her tongue he could feel her heated core rubbing against his already straining erection. Jesus, she really wanted him. From the way she was grinding against him he would say she wanted him now. He was definitely attracted to her, but he never would have expected to get so incredibly lost in the feel of her body.

He was the first to pull away. Breathless he said, "Wait, what are we doing?"

Kissing the side of his neck and nibbling on his ear she whispered, "I can tell you what I'd like to be doing, *cowboy*."

He wanted to laugh. What was it with women when he wore this hat? But God, her tongue. She was causing a fire to race straight down to his cock with every lick and nibble. "Why? Who are you?" *And why the hell do I care?*

"It doesn't matter. Please. I've…never done anything like this before. But I've wanted to. I've fantasized about this, exactly this." She kissed him again. She was so hot for him right now it was a wonder she didn't spontaneously combust.

"You've fantasized? About this?" He had to know more. "What exactly?" Why in God's name did he freaking care? She was sexy as all hell with her chestnut brown hair, gorgeous green eyes and luscious body. *Just give her what she wants already*, he told himself.

Just barely pulling away from his neck, she said "I want to be fucked by a cowboy. I want you to spread me out on the hood of my car and make me come."

Holy Shit! "What if someone sees us? Any number of people drive this road every day. We can't just, oh to hell with it, come here."

Holding onto her tighter he palmed her ass as he walked her over to her car. Leaning over, he gently laid her against the hot metal. He heard her gasp at the slight burn to her skin. He trailed his tongue down into the valley of her cleavage as he reached his hands under her thin t-shirt. Once his fingers made their way underneath her bra, she arched into him. He couldn't take anymore. He had to see her, have her, fuck her.

"Get undressed." His command was half spoken, half groaned.

Ann looked up at him with wide eyes. For some reason she was just realizing what she was doing. What *was* she doing? She should stop this. *Right?* But she didn't listen to her internal warnings.

"What's your name, cowboy?" She asked, but not sure why.

"Get undressed," he said it again as he was unbuttoning his jeans.

For reasons unbeknownst to her, she got off the hood of her car and stripped down to her birthday suit. There she stood, on a barren stretch of road, luckily without another car in sight, as she felt her juices dripping from her pussy.

"Lie down and spread your legs." He waited for her to do as he told her. "God damn, you're gorgeous."

She slid down the hood of the car closer to him as he grabbed her hips and brought her nearer. "Are you sure you want this?"

She nodded as she reached for him. "Yes, please, I want this." She whispered.

He pulled a condom from his wallet and stared at her intently as he sheathed himself. "Play with your tits. Rub them together." He watched her while she began massaging her nipples until the centers jutted outward in invitation. "Oh yeah. God, you're fucking beautiful." His mouth was watering. He bent his head down and captured one of the rosy beauties in his mouth.

"Ooh, mmm." Ann arched into him further.

He was working his tongue over her nipple. From the way her body was writing underneath his ministrations he knew he was. sending tiny little pinpoints of pleasure down to her already aching and throbbing pussy. Never, ever had he been this turned on for a woman before. He had to have her. Now.

* * * *

"Now! Please. I'm so…" She started to beg him, but her plea was interrupted by the feel of him thrusting inside of her. *Oh! Ouch*! *How big was he? This wasn't like she had thought it would be*, she thought to herself as he continued to plunge into her over and over again. It almost hurt.

She could feel her heat. She knew how tight she was, but wasn't prepared for this type of a sensation. She wasn't prepared for this type of discomfort. Never had she felt this amount of pain during sex before. His girth was more than her little body could handle. Looking up at him she felt a small twinge of regret that he was clearly enjoying it so much. Her regret wasn't enough to let him continue though. She blinked and a small tear escaped, sliding down her cheek. As soon as it did she saw the hesitation in him as he slowed his pace. "Are you okay?" He stopped in mid thrust to ask her.

"I…I've never been with anyone so…I'm sorry." How did you tell a man that he was too big? Isn't that like an oxymoron to every woman's fantasy?

Great, this again. "Am I hurting you?"

She nodded, "I'm sorry."

"Fuck!" He screamed in frustration as he pulled out of her.

Getting up off of the car, Ann reached for her clothes and haphazardly put them on. "I'm really sorry."

He yanked up his jeans and buttoned them while looking at her. "Yeah. I know. I've heard it all before." He picked up his hat from the ground and headed towards his truck.

"Wait!" She ran after him. Why did she feel like the world's biggest tease? When she got to him she placed a hand to his arm. "I'm sorry, really I am."

He shrugged. "Forget it. I've become quite accustomed to having to stop in the middle." He glanced at his hand mockingly. "My buddy here will take care of it. See you around."

He got in the truck and sped away as she stood there. She didn't miss the bitterness that etched his voice. She was the one that had started things and then had stopped him midway through. It was a small town. She had no doubt that he would eventually figure out who she was. Surely her name would be written on a bathroom wall somewhere tomorrow. 'For a rotten fuck call Ann,' it would say.

She turned to go toward her car. She was sore. She'd only ever been with two men. If she was honest with herself, they weren't very big, at least not by Playgirl's standards. She didn't get a look at the size of him, but he seemed to stretch her to absolute maximum capacity. He had to be huge, freakishly so. Why else would she have felt so much discomfort? And why with him being gone did she suddenly feel so very empty, with the need to be filled by him all over again?

Ann sat in her car for a moment. How was she going to go to the interview now? She looked disheveled. But it *was* just a Roadhouse. The rowdy bar would probably get its fair share of messy-looking patrons. She reached in her purse and grabbed her brush. Once she was satisfied, she put on some lip gloss and smacked her lips together. *Oh well, it's better than nothing.* It would have to be good enough because she really needed this job. The lady working the front desk at the hotel she was staying at had said the waitresses there made great tips.

* * * *

"Hey boss." Louie yelled from behind the bar.

"I need five minutes!" Quinn snapped as he slammed his office door.

"Alrighty then. I guess I'll go inventory the liquor in the back." Louie walked down the narrow hallway and disappeared behind one of the doors.

Quinn was pissed. After slamming the door, he flung his hat across the office. He needed something, anything, to throw. He was so tired of this happening to him. *Was he that freaking big? I mean, my God.* Weren't women always bitching that their men were too small? Wasn't that why every time he turned on the television there was some sort of an advertisement for male enhancement drugs?

He slumped in his chair and let out a disgusted laugh. He still had the freaking condom on. Damn. He undid his pants and grabbed onto the base of his still throbbing erection as he slowly rolled the condom back off. He glanced up at his door at a sound that caught his attention. And there she was. The gorgeous brown-haired beauty that had begged him to fuck her, and then had just as quickly sent him away.

She stood in the doorway staring at him. Apparently, she hadn't believed his comment about his hand. As he sat there, his legs outstretched, his pants undone and holding his cock she had a wide-eyed look not that much different than that of a deer in headlights.

It was obvious from the sign on the door that he was the manager, but from the look on her face she was just now realizing that. It also seemed that by some cruel twist of fate he had just had sex with the same girl who he was supposed to interview. At that moment, though, the interview and the job were the farthest things from his mind. He sat there and continued to stare at her, still holding his very hard cock. He grinned when he caught her licking her lips. He knew he was large, but he also had been told from previous girlfriends that he also knew how to satisfy a woman. Once they were able to handle him of course. .

"You followed me here?" He asked incredulously, despite knowing what she was really doing there.

"What? No, this is where I was heading before my flat tire. I think we spoke on the phone. I'm Ann." She responded awkwardly. Her eyes never left the site of him fisting himself. She looked as though she wanted nothing more than to drop to her knees and find out just how large he truly was.

"Well that's just great. Well if you'll excuse me, *Ann*, I'm not quite finished yet." He wasn't really going to get himself off, but his pride was hurt, so he lashed out.

"You know. I have more than one fantasy." She told him brazenly.

Finally pulling his hand away from his hardness, he held up his hands. "No. Thanks, but no thanks. I'm not the biggest fan of your fantasies. They always leave me, oh I don't know, wanting more."

She looked genuinely hurt by his comment. "I'm sorry about before. But I could…I mean, if you wanted, I could…"

"Hold on, are you asking what I think you're asking?" *This chick was crazy. First she begs him to fuck her, then she sends him away before either one of them gets to come. Now she's asking if she can give him head? No way is this really happening.*

She didn't say anything as she walked over to him, the whole time not taking her gaze off of his cock. He knew it was jutting out as if insisting that she take it in her mouth.

Quinn watched as she dropped her purse on the floor and fell to her knees in front of him. He should stop her. Lord only knew what she'd do this time. But he didn't. He just watched her and waited.

Ann looked up at him through her eyelashes. Bending over, she slowly swirled her tongue around the tip of his penis and closed her mouth over the head. He had been right. Her leer meant she was dying to taste him. He mentally calmed his nerves as she opened wide to take him deep in her mouth. With a final hiss of breath, he braced himself as she brought her lips tightly around his erection and sucked down on him. The sounds that tore from her throat were animalistic. She sounded like a woman giving her man the most primal of pleasures. Only seconds into it and he gave her his warning.

"Ann, you've got to stop. Oh Jesus. If you don't…fuck yes!" He threw back his head and began pumping into her mouth in earnest.

She was nearly gagging from the attack on her throat. Despite his thrusts, she accepted them and sucked him with everything that she had. He was in awe of the sensations that were pouring through him. He knew he was much larger than most men, and yet she was taking him in as though it was as much for her as it was for him. Her tongue felt like pure indulgence against his cock. He let out a strangled cry as he pumped harder, then finally he hit the back of her throat with such ferocity he thought she would fall over.

He spilled into her mouth as he screamed something even he didn't understand. He was too lost in the erotic sensation of her swallowing every last drop of him. Had she done this to her previous lovers? Had she enjoyed it this much? Never once had he ever had a woman give him such pleasure with her mouth. Now, as she licked her tongue up the underside of his cock, he prayed that he wouldn't have to wait long until she did it again. Oncc would not be enough to have the heat of her mouth give him such ecstasy.

Chapter Two

He stared down at her as she looked up at him. What she had just done to him had felt incredible. Hell, it felt better than incredible, it was amazing! *What should she say now?* She had never given a blow job to a man. The knowledge of her brazen actions hit her full force. Forget about the fact that he was a complete stranger, wasn't there some sort of a customary pat on the head? A proverbial 'thanks, you did good kid' acknowledgement he would give her?

What had she just done? This break up with Larry must be making her insane. Here she was at twenty five years old, a virtual good girl, only been with two men in her entire life, and now in a matter of twenty minutes, she had gotten very naughty with this stranger twice.

"What's your name?" Sure, it really should have been a question that she asked before he came in her mouth, but obviously her priorities were a little messed up.

"Quinn." He lifted his hand to tuck a piece of stray hair behind her ear.

"I…um…I hope you don't think that I did this because of the job." Again, something she really should have discussed before the whole blow job thing.

He shook his head, not saying anything.

The way he was staring at her was making her body heat and flush. He was definitely gorgeous, and he was looking at her like he wanted to eat her alive, despite his recent release. How could she want him so badly when she had felt such discomfort when he was inside of her? Feeling uncomfortable from the way that he was looking at her, she got up and headed for the door. She reached for the handle, suddenly very embarrassed for the way that she had behaved. She was startled by the feel of his warm body pressed up against her back.

"Don't go," he said into her ear.

His softly spoken words caressed her neck. She dropped her head back and let it fall against his chest. "I have to. I can't work here now. I can't believe I just –"

He interrupted her by swiftly turning her around to face him. "I want you." He brought his mouth down to hers and kissed her.

It wasn't sensual or passionate. He kissed her like he was a mad man in a frenzy. She felt the door to his office meet her back in a loud thud. She should have pushed him away. She knew she couldn't handle his size. *But damn if what he was doing with his tongue didn't feel so good.* When he reached his hand down to cup her bottom she instinctively ground against him. Surprised, she looked at him. "You're…"

He smirked, "Yeah I am. I told you I wanted you."

But so soon after? How could he be hard again so soon after she had gone to such lengths to make sure that he was taken care of? This was crazy. She knew it was.

"Listen, I know I started this. But I really don't do things like this." She tried to tear her eyes away from his gaze. What were his eyes? Blue or black? She wasn't sure, they were so dark.

"Oh? It seems to me that you do things just like this. Seeing as you just did," he said rather smugly.

He was right and she knew it, but his arrogance at her brazen behavior pissed her off. She was not some floozy who did this sort of thing with whoever was handy. And she certainly was not easy. She would have continued the silent argument with herself if he hadn't interrupted her.

"Come on, give me another chance. I bet I can make it feel good this time. I bet I can make you come." He whispered the last words as he bent his head to kiss her again.

And there it was. He suddenly was not so attractive after all. What was it with men that thought they could give you exactly what you needed? Hell, if they were as good as they thought they were, women wouldn't need fantasy lists. Larry had been the exact same way. So incredibly convinced of his sexual prowess that he had stopped trying to please her. Maybe it had been partially her fault. If she hadn't invested so much energy into faking those orgasms at the beginning of their relationship maybe he would have been more in tuned to what a tedious and boring lover he truly was. And maybe she was bashing him slightly more than necessary, but she was entitled. After all, he had been screwing around on her for months.

"Come on, Ann. Let me fuck you, just like you wanted me to. You felt so good when I was inside you. I want to make you feel good, too." He was grinding his hips against her, reinforcing his request.

She was in awe of how turned on he could be so soon after she had done what she'd done. And what was his tongue doing to her skin? She could swear that she heard her skin sizzling with each and every lick. She couldn't do this. *He's too large*. There was just no way. As if her silence was an invitation, she felt herself being picked up and carried to his desk. After being set down on the edge she felt him pull down her jean shorts, taking her panties along with them. *Stop*, she whispered inside her head. *Why wasn't she stopping him?* Maybe it was because no matter how big she knew he was, she couldn't fight this aching need she had to feel him inside of her again. Surely she must be sadistic.

He had just put another condom on as he spread her legs apart and positioned himself at her entrance. He removed one hand and gently brushed his fingertips along her cheek. "You are so damn gorgeous."

She blushed. *Why?* She got naked, in broad daylight no less, on the hood of her car, and got down on her knees and sucked on his beautiful cock until he came in her mouth. But for some reason him telling her that she was gorgeous made her feel embarrassed.

Quinn leaned over and kissed her. This time it was passionate. He wasn't attacking her with his tongue, rather enticing her with it. She reached her arms up to grasp onto his shoulders. She heard a whimper, and knew that it came from her. *God, she wanted him too! Why? Why was the need to be filled with him so strong?*

He pulled away from her just slightly. His lips just barely touching hers, he said, "Don't stop me this time. Please. I know I'm big, but give it a chance. Give me a chance." For reasons unknown to her she was overwhelmed with emotion at his last request. Give *him* a chance? Had he been with many women before who had turned him away because of his size? She didn't know him, but felt sure that never once had he had to beg another woman for a chance. *Why was he doing so now? And why with her?*

She nodded. "Okay." It was barely a whisper, but he heard her loud and clear.

She noticed that rather than take her quickly like he had earlier, he slowly eased himself inside of her. He watched as she winced in discomfort when he only buried half of his hardness inside of her. *Damn.* It still hurt, but she couldn't ignore the sensations that were rolling inside of her.

He quietly asked her, "Do you want me to stop?"

Her heart was pounding. Despite the initial discomfort, she had to admit that it wasn't nearly as bad as it had been earlier. There was a little burn as he stretched her. But that burn was quickly being replaced by tingling. She shook her head."Kiss me like you did before."

He didn't answer her with words, but with actions. He leaned over and gave her what she wanted. The motion caused him to slide a little bit further inside of her. She tensed for a moment underneath the pressure of taking more of him. He almost pulled away and out of her until she stopped him. She reached her hands around his hips and held his body to hers.

"Is it okay?" He cautiously asked her.

She was beginning to relax now. She could feel the walls of her pussy throbbing with his invasion, but it was no longer a discomfort or a pain. It was a warm fluttery feeling. *Oh yeah.* She could still feel her nerves tingling as she accepted him further into her body. "Quinn. I need more." She surprised herself at her demand.

He looked at her in shock. "Are you sure?"

In answer to his question, she reached her legs around his back and locked her ankles together, bringing him closer to her. "Ooh…yes." The sound escaped from her mouth without her knowledge.

As he looked down at her, she knew her flush of arousal was evident. She was moaning and writhing against him. There should be no question of whether or not she was actually enjoying it.

"Ann?" He said her name, as though seeking an answer he wasn't sure he'd gotten.

She opened her eyes to stare up at him. She smiled. "Quinn, take me. You feel so good."

He sank all the way inside of her. She saw the restraint on his face when he was finally buried completely in her. It looked like he almost bit his own tongue to keep from letting all of the expletives that were swirling around in his head from falling from his mouth. Damn, she felt so tight, so stretched. She wondered what it felt like to him. Did she feel like a sweet vice, grasping him snugly?

He looked at her intently. She wasn't asking him to stop, but she knew he was waiting for her to. She could feel the insides of her pussy trembling. She wanted him to rock in and out of her, but it was obvious that he was worried that if he did too much it would become too uncomfortable for her and she would make him stop again.

"Quinn, please." *God, he felt so good.* How could she have stopped him earlier?

With a look of sincerity, he looked into her eyes and spoke softly. "I don't want to hurt you."

"No, I swear it feels good. I just needed time." She wasn't waiting for him any longer. She started to rock against him, slowly stroking his hardness in and out of her.

Quinn must have reached his breaking point because he was unable to hold back anymore. He began to meet her demands, and with every deep thrust she gasped and felt her pussy throb even more. She wondered how she felt like a fifteen year old virgin, but still felt like this was the best sex she'd ever had.

"Oh God, Quinn. Touch me!" She screamed.

He brought his hand down to her clit and groaned when he felt how completely soaking wet she truly was. Using his thumb he massaged the swollen nub, causing her body to thrash from side to side. In all of his life, he had never seen anything quite so erotic. She was now pinching her nipples as she writhed beneath his touch.

"Yes. Quinn, yes, harder, faster! Oh God…yes…ooh…" She exploded with the most intense orgasm she had ever felt in her entire life. An extreme heat flared through her body and held onto her while tiny fireworks went off inside, shooting lightning bolts of pleasure down to her womb as her orgasm flowed over him.

Quinn was lost. Her pussy was contracting around his cock and clutching onto him in the sweetest sensation of euphoria. He threw his head back and grunted, screamed and shouted all at the same time. Although he wasn't sure how, he came like it had been weeks since he'd had any release. The orgasm continued to rip through him for several moments as his cock twitched inside of her with every spurt of his semen.

Finally he was done, finished and completely exhausted. He was leaning on top of her, heaving, trying to catch his breath. He was still inside of her and could feel the aftershocks of her orgasm. It was almost as if she was vibrating around him. His oxygen level was slowly starting to return to normal as he propped himself up enough to look down at her. "Are you okay?"

Ann looked at him. "Yeah. I can't believe…that felt so good."

Did it ever. "Are you sure? I didn't hurt you, did I?"

She smiled at him as she brought her hand up to run her fingers through his hair. "No. It was amazing. And I'm not just saying that, either. I've never felt anything like that before."

Quinn used every amount of strength he had to keep from grinning. *Amazing?* No one had ever told him that before. And truth be told, he was more than a little bitter when it came to sex and women. He had been told by so many women that he was too big, and it pissed him off. He didn't want to hurt any of them, but just to make them feel good. *To hell with it,* he pushed the past memories aside and smiled at her.

"You really liked it? It wasn't too…much?"

"Uh uh." Her smirk reinforced her answer.

"Boss?" Lenny yelled from the other side of the door.

Quinn felt Ann tense underneath him at the surprise. "Yeah Lenny?" Did he lock the door? He didn't think so.

"You all right in there? I was in the back room, thought I heard you shout."

Quinn and Ann both laughed. "Yeah, I'm fine. I just stubbed my toe." He shrugged, what was he gonna say? *Oh yeah. Sorry to worry you, Larry. I just had the best orgasm of my entire life while I was buried deep inside an incredibly gorgeous woman.*

"Okay, just checking. Listen, I'm all done, I'm gonna head out for lunch. You want anything to eat?"

Again, Quinn and Ann laughed. They were both thinking the same thing. "No, I think I'll find something here to munch on." His answer sent Ann into such hysterics that Quinn had to cover her mouth to muffle her sounds.

"All right then. See you in an hour." Lenny shuffled his feet down the hallway.

Quinn stared at her and shook his head grinning, "Who are you?"

She bunched her brows together. "I told you, Ann."

He chuckled, "Not your name. I mean *who* are you? I've never met anyone like you before."

"I hope that's a good thing."

"I'm still inside you, aren't I? Yeah, it's a good thing."

"So, does this mean I aced the interview, or blew it?" She gave him a seductive smirk and wink.

This time Quinn laughed so hard he slipped out of her.

"What's so funny? I was only teasing." His laughter was contagious because despite her current position she was giggling right along with him.

"Oh, you definitely blew it, alright." He shook his head as he held his hand out to her. "You want to grab some lunch?"

Ann was pulling up her shorts quickly and asked him nervously, "I…Do you have a bathroom?"

"Yeah, behind that door." He motioned with his hand to a small door in the corner of his office.

He watched her as she went inside and closed the door. He had to admit, he thought it was cute how she could all of a sudden seem bashful. He waited while she cleaned herself up and wondered who she was, besides her name. He'd lived in Oakdale almost his whole life and knew almost everyone. She obviously was new in town, which meant she probably hadn't met many people yet. This was fine by him, because he had every intention of seeing her again. In very much the same way he had minutes ago, with her naked and writhing beneath him in pleasure. His thoughts were interrupted when the door opened and she walked out.

Ann strode over and picked up her purse from where she had dropped it on the floor, right before she'd—done what she'd done. She turned to him and quickly turned away, unable to meet his gaze. "Are you okay?" He wondered aloud. He didn't miss how quickly she turned away from him.

"Yeah, I'm…embarrassed, I guess you could say. I wasn't kidding earlier. I've never done anything like this before. I don't know what came over me." She smiled at him. The embarrassment covered her face in the form of red cheeks.

He walked to her, hating that she was feeling regrets. He definitely wasn't. "If you think I think badly of you, I don't."

She looked up at him as he put his hands on her shoulders. "Really? I mean, I know that you're a nice guy and, well, I guess I don't really know that. But you seem like a nice guy and you don't have to give me a bunch of sweet words. I mean we've already, you know. So, it's not like you have to try to be all nice to me."

Quinn was shocked by her low opinion of both him and herself. "Is that what you think? Listen, what we did was incredible and yes it is over now. But I was kind of hoping I could see you again sometime." He held up his hand when she started to speak. "Outside of work, because I won't be hiring you."

Quinn had to stop her from the obvious rush of fury that swept through her. She hadn't been with him to get the job. But the idea that he screwed her, and now refused to hire her, seemed like the ultimate insult. "How dare –"

"Hold on. Hear me out." He waited for her to close her dropped open mouth before continuing, "I like you. And this job calls for a woman that can handle men grabbing at her and making all sorts of lewd comments. The guy from the side of the road earlier, he's a regular."

"I'm quite capable of taking care of myself, and for the record, I find it completely deplorable that you can – umph." She was silenced by his mouth pressed against hers. His lips were gentle and undemanding when they brushed against hers.

Satisfied that he had stunned her into silence, Quinn pulled away from her. "Now, as I was trying to explain, I like you. I was hoping that I would get to see you again. But I don't want it to be while some jerk is grabbing your ass. So, my brother and I have a restaurant in town, nothing fancy, just a little steak joint. We need a hostess for a few shifts during the week and alternating weekends."

Quinn watched as her expression changed from shocked to inquisitive. "So, what do you say? You interested?"

She cocked her eyebrow up at him. "Let me see if I've got this straight. You just met me, but the idea of another man grabbing my ass bothers you so much you won't hire me here, but you'll give me a job at your restaurant. Does that about sum it up?" She waited for him to answer.

"Yep, that pretty much covers it."

A large and amused grin formed on her face. "You don't even know me. What if I'm a horrible employee?"

He shrugged, "You're good at other things. I assume you'll be good at all things you do."

"Pretty big assumption." She pointed out.

"Does that mean you don't want the job?" He wanted desperately to kiss her again but restrained himself.

This time she shrugged, "That depends."

"On what?"

"Would I have to sleep with you?" She said teasing, but waited to hear his answer.

"You won't have to. But I sure as hell hope you do." He winked at her. "Now do you want the job or not, because I'm dying to kiss you again." Quinn didn't wait for her answer as he took possession of her mouth with his.

Chapter Three

"You think you can handle all that?" Derek asked her.

"Yeah, it sounds easy enough. Will you be around if I need help?" Ann asked, knowing she wouldn't.

"Yeah, I'll be in the back. We're uploading a new payroll system. Just let me know if you need anything." He smiled at her.

"Okay, thanks." Ann watched Quinn's brother walk away. He was the polar opposite of his brother. While Quinn had dark hair and tan skin with dark eyes, Derek was blonde haired, blue eyed and fair skinned. Other than their obvious similarities in the height department, they looked nothing alike. If Quinn hadn't told her they were brothers, she would never have believed it.

Ann spent the next several minutes getting acquainted with her cute new work station. She had a little podium, a clipboard, a holder for the menus and her own cordless phone. She was a hostess at a little steak restaurant and for some reason, she felt like an executive who was just given the corner office of the top floor. It was just a silly, menial job, but she felt great. Well, it was possible that she felt great because last night, hours after Quinn had bought her lunch, he had come to her hotel room and made her feel just as incredible as he had when she was spread out on his desk. A warm flush ran up her face at the memory of it.

"What are you thinking about?"

Abruptly, Ann turned to see Quinn standing there grinning. He was wearing that cowboy hat again. Something about that hat made her knees go weak with need. She pointed her finger at him. "You scared me."

"I only scared you because you were lost in thought." He came to her and wrapped his arms around her. "You gonna tell me what has your face so red?"

She twinkled her eyes at him. "No, I'm not."

"Fine, be a tease. So, how's it going?" He peeked around the restaurant, wondering where his uptight brother was.

"Derek's in the back, if that's who you're looking for."

"Good, then I can do this." Quinn pulled off his hat and set it on the podium as he leaned over to kiss her. He couldn't seem to get enough of her. After he left her last night, he found himself lying in bed with a hard on. He didn't even know why he left. Being a macho guy, he thought he would look stupid if he asked to stay. Guys weren't supposed to want to stay and cuddle, which surprisingly was what he wanted to do. Besides, he knew he had to go. He had been so caught up in the act with her last night that he almost let some of his secrets spill. She had been talking to him about her fantasy, the one about the cowboy who rescues her on the side of the road, when he almost let one of his come out. He knew then he had to high tail it out of there. It was bad enough he was too big to be comfortable for most women. But now that he finally had one that he really liked, and they had great sex together, he wasn't about to jeopardize it just because he had a few fetishes.

"Wow," Ann said when she pulled away. "You are really good at that."

In his best Elvis accent he said, "Thank you, thank you very much."

"Oh Jesus, you doing Elvis again?" Derek asked from across the restaurant.

Quinn turned to his brother. "Yep, I sound just like him, huh?"

"Hardly. Listen, this program keeps giving me an error every time I get it about 50% loaded. It do that to you at the Roadhouse?" Derek asked.

Quinn shook his head. “No, did you look at the manual that came with it?”

Derek tilted his head in mock amusement, “No asshole, I just figured it would magically work. Don’t little fairies come and install everything while we sleep? Yes, I read the damn manual.”

“All right, fine.” He turned to Ann. “I’ll be back. I need to go help him with this. He gets kind of high strung sometimes.”

“Sure, of course.”

Quinn walked away, but not before giving her a quick wink.

Ann didn’t see Quinn come out of the office. She assumed she had missed him though because his hat was gone and they had gotten very busy with a lunch rush. Which she admitted to herself was actually kind of fun. She enjoyed all the people that came in. They all seemed to be regulars that knew each other well. When they asked who she was, they welcomed her warmly with kind words of encouragement for her new job. She smiled to herself as she thought she was really going to like it. Lord knew she already had a soft spot for her boss, well at least one of them anyway.

Ann sat down in a chair after the last of the lunch customers had left. They were so busy that she took to bussing tables to help the wait-staff keep up with the steady flow of patrons. She closed her eyes for only a moment when she opened them to the smell of something wonderful. She looked up and saw Derek.

“You were running pretty hectic there for a while. I thought you’d be hungry.”

She looked at the small pie in front of her. “What is it?”

“My specialty. You’ve heard of beef pot pie. Well this is like that, only with tender marinated sirloin and my own spices.” He motioned with his hands. “Go ahead, try it. It’s good, I promise.”

Ann reached for a fork and smiled. “It smells heavenly.”

Derek watched her as she took a bite and moaned. “Good?”

“Mmm hmm. This is fabulous,” she told him honestly.

"I'm glad you like it." He got up from the table and started to turn away, but stopped himself, "You know Ann, I love my brother."

Ann placed the fork down, suddenly feeling like she was under a microscope. "Obviously. Why wouldn't you?"

"I guess what I'm trying to say is…well, he hasn't had the best of luck with women. I don't want to see him hurt. He seems to like you."

"Really?" God, she sounded like a school girl. *Really? Do you really think he likes me? Geez.*

"Yeah, I think he does. So, just be good to him, huh? He's a good guy." Derek looked clearly uncomfortable saying it. His need to protect his brother was apparent. "Quinn hasn't had it easy over the years. It's left him…bitter I guess you could say. I just don't want him to be hurt again. Treat him right okay?" Ann nodded, knowing that while he was being nice, there was also a warning somewhere in his request. "I will, Derek," she said as he started to turn away, "I like him, too. More than I think is normal after knowing him for only a day." She smiled, hoping he knew she was telling the truth.

"Good." Changing the serious mood he said, "Now hurry up, we're not paying you to sit on your tush and eat my wonderful food." And he walked back into his office.

Ann ate her sirloin pot pie and smiled. She was definitely going to like it here. The only question was, Larry who? She giggled.

Hours later, Derek was arguing with Ann in the back office. "I'm the boss. So, I can make you."

Ann laughed, "Come on Derek, that's stupid. Look how busy we are."

Derek rolled his eyes. "There are labor laws, you know."

"In Oakdale. Really? Come on. I'm not tired, and I'm having fun. The people here are great. Let me stay? Please." Ann asked him with complete sincerity. It was stupid, but she had such a good time today and she wasn't really that tired. What else was she going to do? Go sit in her hotel room and watch reruns of Will & Grace? It's not like she could entertain herself with more mind blowing orgasms with Quinn. He would be at the Roadhouse until late tonight.

Derek sighed. “Fine, but you’re coming in late tomorrow.”

“Deal,” she said as she shook his hand and ran back out to her little podium.

She smiled when she got back up to the front of the small restaurant. “Mr. and Mrs. Tollson, weren’t you just here five hours ago?”

Mrs. Tollson gave her husband the evil eye and said, “I ain’t cooking for someone that doesn’t appreciate me.”

Mr. Tollson looked to the heavens above, for either encouragement or to be struck dead. “For the last time, Martha, I told you I didn’t mean it the way it sounded. You take everything so dang personal. I’d ask if it was your time of month but I know you’re past that point in your life so—”

Ann listened in horror. He had not just said that to his wife in front of all of these people. People they knew. “Ah, Mrs. Tollson, where did you get those earrings? My God, they’re gorgeous!”

Mrs. Tollson tore her death stare away from her husband and looked at Ann. “You really like them? I bought them at Betty’s Boutique just around the corner.”

“I hope they have more. They look great.” Ann reached over and touched the small silver dangles.

“Thank you dear. Do we have long to wait?”

Ann checked her list. “No, I’d say about ten or fifteen minutes tops.”

“That’ll be fine.” Mr. Tollson said. “You know honey, those are beautiful earrings. They do a great job hiding how big your ears really are.” He told her with a smile, proud of himself for being so smooth with the compliment. His smile quickly turned to a frown when both his wife and all of the surrounding couples gasped in horror.

“Oh Jesus, now what? What’d I say?” He asked them all.

"Mr. Tollson," Ann gently took his arm, guiding him away from the onlookers. "Perhaps it's not really a compliment if you mention a flaw. You know what I mean?"

Mr. Tollson bunched his brows together as he pondered her advice. "So, say something nice and leave it at that?"

Ann laughed. "Exactly."

"Well, hell. Why didn't somebody tell me this sooner? Twenty three years of marriage, she never said anything. How am I supposed to know?"

Ann patted his arm. "Well, now you do. So, just remember to, I don't know, think before you speak. Okay?"

Mr. Tollson nodded at her. "Thanks. I like you, you're nice."

Surprised, Ann blushed. "Thank you, Mr. Tollson."

"You're seeing one of the Travis boys, aren't you?" He asked her.

"Yes, Quinn, but it's still fairly new so I don't really want word getting around that—" She was startled by the three couples laughing at her.

"Honey," Mrs. Tollson told her, "You should have thought of that before you let Quinn into your hotel room at three o'clock in the morning. That Sandi who works the front desk can't talk without spreading rumors."

Ann was embarrassed. "So, who knows then?"

One of the other men waiting, Mr. Rollins piped in, "Well, let's see. There's me, you, them," he said pointing around at the other people in the restaurant. "Then, there are the people that came in contact with Sandi, then the people that came in contact with those people, and the people that came in contact with those people, and so on and so on. So I guess I'd say probably the whole town."

Ann's face turned red with embarrassment. "Great."

"Don't worry, dear. Quinn's a good boy. He comes from good stock." Mrs. Tollson told her. "He'll treat you right. His mama raised him good."

They all had a good laugh at Ann's expense. While she wasn't angry with them, she just felt somewhat uneasy that so many people knew that she had slept with Quinn, especially since she only got to town yesterday morning. That would do wonders for her reputation in a town this size. And to think she chose a small town because she thought she wanted to get away from all the bull that went along with living in the city. Unfortunately, she didn't realize that the country had bull too, just a different kind.

Hours later, Derek lifted the last chair to rest on top of the table. "That's it, we're all done."

"Whew. I *am* tired *now*. I can't believe how busy you guys get."

Derek sighed as he sat down. "Yeah, it was a good idea to open this place. It's the only place in town that serves a decent steak and potatoes meal. Everything else is just diners and sandwich shops."

Ann sat down across from Derek and rested her chin on her palm. "How long have you and Quinn been in business together?"

Derek squinted his eyes, thinking. "We just have the restaurant together. We have different mothers. Our dad had some issues with fidelity. Wasn't the best role model for me and Quinn. He loved both of our mothers in his own way. But he just had some major difficulties with the whole faithfulness thing. I'm only a few years older than Quinn. Shortly after I was born my parents got a divorce. My Dad's jealousy ruined things. Which is ironic, seeing as how monogamy wasn't one of his personality traits. Anyway, then he got together with Quinn's mom. They fell in love and got married. Problem is he never stopped loving my mom. It was hard. He was a tough old bastard. He broke both of their hearts on a daily basis. Always promising to leave one for the other and vice versa. It made the holidays really uncomfortable."

Ann's eyes widened at that. "Holidays? My God, you guys spent the holidays together?"

Derek laughed, realizing his mistake. "Oops. Yeah, probably should have told you that part. Our moms were sisters."

Ann's mouth dropped open. "No way!"

He laughed some more. "Way. Anyhow, the Roadhouse was the business my Aunt Connie and dad had started, so it went to Quinn. He never did much with my mom. So when I got out of the military because of…well, it doesn't matter. But when I got out, we decided to start this little venture. Going on five years now."

"Five years. How old are you?" Ann instantly knew what she'd said. "And that was incredibly rude. Sorry."

"No. It's fine. I'm thirty. Quinn's twenty-seven."

She nodded, hating that she had had sex with Quinn four times in the past twenty four hours and had no idea how old he was.

"Listen, why don't you get out of here? I just need to lock up and I'll be leaving, too. Oh shoot, now that *was* rude. I'm sorry. Wait here. Let me get the keys and I'll walk you out."

"Thanks," she said and meant it. She couldn't remember the last time she was around a man that actually put her safety ahead of whatever was going on with him at the time.

Derek came back with the keys and he set the alarm before they exited the restaurant. They said their good nights and she headed for her hotel. She wanted to take a hot bath and relax her aching feet. And maybe, she hoped, if she was a good little girl, Quinn would come and surprise her later. She hadn't talked to him since earlier that day so they hadn't made any plans. But a girl could hope, couldn't she?

Chapter Four

Ann woke up and stretched like a contented cat. She was a little sore, but she didn't really care though. It had been worth it. Quinn brought melted chocolate, strawberries and whipped cream for them to share in bed. "It's our one week anniversary," he told her. She couldn't help but giggle, they had only met one week ago and they were pretty much inseparable. She rolled over and gently played with Quinn's chest hair. Resisting the urge to nibble on him, she gave him a small kiss instead.

Quinn stirred, squinting against the light. "Oh," he groaned. "Is it morning already?"

"Yep. Are you gonna sleep all day?"

"Just fifteen more minutes." He rolled over.

She couldn't resist the urge to toy with him. "All right, it's just that I was thinking, you, me, the shower. Whatever though, it's no biggie."

Quinn rolled back over. Opening just one eye he looked at her and grinned. "What'd you have in mind?"

Ann smiled at him. "Use your imagination big boy." And she strode into the bathroom.

She knew Quinn was no fool. There was no way he was going to pass up her little invitation. He got out of bed and got into the shower right behind her. Wrapping his arms around her, he pulled her against his chest. His cock brushed against her ass, effectively waking him up for duty.

Ann pulled her arms up and over her head to reach for him behind her. The sensation of him rubbing his hardness against her rear was strange. Actually, not just strange, it was driving her crazy. She didn't know why. Sure she had heard of some women letting their men do things to them there. Surely she wasn't one of those sex crazed women. It's not like she would ever do something like that. Right?

"Damn, you're so sexy Ann." Quinn was kissing the side of her neck and grinding himself against her backside. "Do you have any idea what you do to me?"

Was he talking? She wasn't sure, because she was distracted. She was absolutely and one hundred percent on fire for him. No matter how many times they were together she was always surprised at how much he drove her desire to new extremes. "Quinn, oh…Quinn. You feel so good." She moaned to him.

Quinn was rubbing her clit, massaging her into orgasm. She loved how he was able to make her come so easily. She wished she could share everything with him. He was so amazing. They fit so well together. In more ways than one, and when he was deep inside of her, oh God, it was freaking incredible.

"Do you know what I want to do to you?" He asked her.

She whimpered, but didn't answer him. She was simply too lost in his touch.

"I want to bend you over honey. Jesus, I can't get over how amazing you are." He was losing control as she writhed against him. "I want to fuck you from behind."

Ann stilled. "What?" She whispered.

He stopped and hesitated before asking, "Have you ever done it before?" He knew from their previous talks that she'd only ever been with two other men.

"Which way? I mean, you said from behind, but how do you mean?"

He nodded in acknowledgment, apparently understanding her apprehension. "Not that babe. I still want to be inside your sweet, tight pussy. I just want to do it from behind. That's all."

Relief washed over her. No matter how much she might feel a little twinge of excitement at the idea of the other way, she didn't think she could ever actually go through with it. "Oh. Well, no I've never done it that way before."

He seemed surprised by her admission. Was that sort of thing normal? Her inexperience left her with little or no basis for comparison when it came to men.

When she didn't answer right away he asked again. "Well? What do you think? Will you let me?"

She wanted to, but would it hurt? He was already so big. "How would it feel?" She asked him nervously.

He eased her anxiety, by kissing the side of her neck. "It will feel good, I promise. I'll make sure you feel good honey." He rubbed himself in the seam of her ass again, his hardness swelling even more than before. "Let me, baby. Please."

Like she could really say no to him. He was an amazing lover. So if he said it would feel good, she knew he wasn't lying. She didn't answer him, she just leaned over and held onto the edge of the tub for support.

Quinn stood there staring at her new position. She was bent clear over with her legs slightly parted. Her ass was stuck up in the air in invitation for him to take her. He gently massaged the soft globes of her cheeks and bit back a curse when he caught sight of her tight little hole.

The curiosity of what he must be thinking made her even hotter. It was a good thing she had no idea what she really wanted him to do to her. Sure, she wanted him to be inside of her. That was the truth. But the idea of him taking her in her most intimate tiny opening, oh the thought of it alone was enough to send her over the edge.

Unsure of herself and very aware of the vulnerable position she was in, Ann turned her head slightly, "Quinn? Is this right? Should I be like this?"

"Yeah, honey. Just like that." He placed a gentle kiss to the small of her back. "God you're beautiful, Annie."

Annie? He had never called her Annie before. Ooh, what was he doing with his tongue? And, oh my, is that? "Oh Quinn."

Quinn ran his finger along the seam of her ass and just barely pressed the tip against her tiny hole. "Do you like that honey? Does it feel good?"

Yes. No. I mean, yes. "Quinn…what are you doing?"

She wasn't ready for this. He knew it. And no way was he going to mess up what they had going by pushing her too far. "Sorry, baby. I couldn't resist. I'll stop."

No. It felt good! Silently, she thanked herself for not saying that aloud. What was wrong with her? How could she be…*oh yes.* He slid inside of her while she had been waging her private battle.

Quinn was lost to her. Not just the sex. Lord knew that was amazing. But every time he was with her, bringing their bodies together, he always felt this tight feeling in his chest. It hurt, but at the same time left him feeling so warm inside. What was happening to him? Was it merely because she was sensual enough to take all of him, or was it the woman herself? He had to know, but at the same time, he didn't care. Because when it came right down to it, it wouldn't change anything. He would still have to have her. He would still miss her whenever she wasn't around.

Quinn reached around and palmed her full, round breasts. They felt so good in his hands, overfilling them. As the water continued to beat down on their bodies, he rhythmically slid in and out of her as he listened to her gasp with each and every thrust. He knew she was close. Only one week ago they had started their little affair, and he already knew everything about her body. How it responded, what it liked.

He looked down at her from the position he was in. Well, he didn't know everything he realized. He didn't know what it was like to take her in the place that was driving him wild. In the tiny puckered whole that centered her round ass. She always felt so tight around him anyway. But the idea of how tight she would be there. *Oh Jesus.* He couldn't hold back anymore. He began to vigorously thrust in and out of her, relishing in her moans of pleasure with every hard slam against the deepest part of her body. Quinn reached down and fingered her clit. She was closer than he thought. Because two little swipes with his finger she lost it. He slammed into her once more and went with her, basking in the feeling of the walls of her pussy convulsing around his cock. *Heaven.* That was the only way to describe what making love to her was. *Heaven. Wait. What? Did he just think about 'making love'? Oh hell, he was freaking falling in love with her.* He never wanted to settle down with one woman. And here he was falling in love with someone after only one week. *He should really be more upset about this, shouldn't he?*

Leaning over her, waiting for the rolling waves of pleasure to subside, he thought about his epiphany. He loved her? What would that mean? He smiled. It would mean many more happy times, just like this one, he thought. *Loving Ann, Annie. Yeah, not such a bad thing.* He could definitely get used to this.

"Quinn. That was amazing!" Ann said breathlessly over her shoulder. "You are lucky we had that talk yesterday."

He eased out of her and turned her around. "Oh shoot, honey. I'm sorry. I got carried away." He had forgotten to put a condom on. Just yesterday they had toyed with the idea of trying it without one. She told him that she was healthy, and he knew that he was. That in combination with the fact that she was on birth control had made them consider it. Apparently, he had decided to make the decision without her. Because without even asking her, he had come inside of her without a condom on. "Are you mad at me?"

She smiled at him. "I suppose I should be. But I'm not. We talked about it. And I…well I know it's only been a week, but I feel like I can trust you."

She would have no idea how it made him feel to hear her say that. “You can trust me, Annie.” He kissed her, passionately.

She cocked an eyebrow at him. “Annie? You said that a few minutes ago. You’ve never called me that before.”

Quinn framed her small face with his large hands. “I like calling you Annie. I like everything about you.” *Okay, so maybe he hadn’t said love, but he wanted to make sure she knew just how important she was to him.*

Ann blushed. “Quinn, you’re embarss—oh! That’s cold.” She jumped out of the shower with Quinn following.

They were both drying off quickly, while laughing. “So much for a shower, huh?” He told her.

Shivering she said, “It’s this damn hotel. You can’t get more than ten minutes of hot water. It’s ridiculous.” Wrapping a towel around herself she walked over to him and put her arms around him. “Warm me up.”

Quinn obliged her and pulled her close. “Maybe you shouldn’t stay here anymore.”

She laughed. “Seeing as how it’s the only hotel in Oakdale, where do you propose I stay?”

“My place.” It was a simple statement. With giant ramifications. Where in the hell had that come from? But if he was to be completely honest with himself, it didn’t sound like such a bad idea. It would be like that MTV slogan. All music, all the time. Only this would be all Ann, all the time. He grinned at his own little joke. But then he realized that she hadn’t answered him yet. “What? Cat got your tongue?”

Ann swallowed the lump that had formed in her throat. Had he just said what she thought he did? “Do you mean, like live with you?” As soon as she said it, she wished she hadn’t. Of course he hadn’t meant that. They’d only known each other a week. It’s not like they were in love or anything. At least she didn’t think so. Sure, she was ridiculously happy whenever he was around. And making love to him was—woah, wait a minute. Making love? They started out with just an urgent need to fuck each other senseless. Why would she now be thinking of making love? *Oh crap!* She *was* falling in love with him. *Which of course meant that he would soon turn into a loser. Just like Larry and Brett. Great!* And she was having such a good time too.

"Hello in there. Where'd you go?" He asked because of her faraway look.

"Sorry, I shouldn't have jumped to conclusions. What did you have in mind?" *Play it cool. Don't let on that you have feelings for him. That's when they start to change and stop appreciating you.*

"Actually you had it right. Live with me. Move in with me." He was dead serious and none too happy when she started to laugh.

The intent way he was staring at her was making her nervous. She had to do something to break up the heaviness of the mood. So she started to giggle, as though he actually was joking. Although she was all too aware from the look on his face that he didn't find it funny at all. "I'm sorry Quinn. Were you being sincere?"

If she had smacked him clear across the face he didn't think it would hurt as much as her humorous outlook on something that was so important to him. "Yeah, I was. But nevermind. I get it." He stormed out of the room in all of his naked glory.

Oh no, her nervous reaction had caused her to act stupid, which now has only made him angry. She ran in after him. "Quinn, I'm sorry. I seriously thought you were joking around."

"Clearly." He pulled his pants up, forgetting about his briefs and sat in the chair to pull his boots on.

He was leaving. It wasn't that he was just leaving, but that he was leaving angry. Never a good combination in a man. Or a woman for that matter. "Quinn, please don't go. I'm sorry."

How could she tell him that she had laughed out of fear? If he knew how she really felt, she would surely lose him. Whether it was to other women, or lack of respect, it would happen anyway. It was inevitable. It had happened with both of her previous boyfriends. And if it happened with two others, than surely it would happen with—wait. Suddenly she remembered an old expression. Something about the third time being the charm. *Could it be true?* She better decide quickly, because he had just pulled on his t-shirt and was heading for the door.

"Quinn, stop! I panicked okay. It's because I was scared, can you try and understand that?" There she'd said it.

Quinn stopped in his tracks. He was standing in the doorway, ready to walk out when he heard her. He turned to face her. "Scared about what?"

Ann rolled her eyes and looked up at the ceiling while expelling a huge breath. She looked back at him and went to sit on the edge of the bed.

Quinn watched her. She looked torn up about something. He closed the door and went to sit next to her. He wished she didn't look so damn sexy in that towel. Because he was still a little mad at her. And it was really hard to stay mad at someone when you wanted to ravish them. "What's wrong? Did I push too far too soon?"

Ann looked at him and laughed. "I'm sorry. I never realized how silly I get when I get nervous."

Quinn couldn't help himself. He pulled her to sit in his lap and held her. "Did I make you nervous when I asked you to move in with me?"

She nodded. "I'm sorry. I just don't want to screw this up." Looking up at him she said, "I really like you."

This time Quinn laughed. "Well, I should hope so. We have sex every day." He laughed harder but was forced to calm himself. She looked so serious.

"No. I mean I *really* like you." She shrugged. "And I have a history of screwing up a relationship every time I really start to like someone."

He didn't like that. He didn't want her comparing him to her past boyfriends. He took his forefinger and thumb and brought her chin up so that she would be forced to look at him. "Ann, how could you screw anything up? You're amazing."

She placed a hand to his cheek. "Quinn, that's sweet of you to say. But I really don't want you to regret anything with me. I don't want you to rush into something and then wish you could take it back."

"Geez, Ann. You're overanalyzing this. I like you and you like me. We have amazing, mind-blowing sex, so just move in with me. If it doesn't work out then you can come back here, no hard feelings. But before you dismiss it entirely, why don't you give it a chance?"

God, she wanted to. The idea of going to bed with him every night and waking up to him every morning was fantastic. Well, they already did that now, but then he always had to go home. To live under the same roof would definitely be different. *Should she? Could she?*

"Come on, what do you say?"

She stared at him. He was so handsome. And she absolutely loved being around him. Oh, what should she do?

"Annie, please." His whispered plea came out more desperate than he had intended it to. But he couldn't help it. Suddenly the idea of her living with him was of the utmost importance. Almost as if he couldn't be truly happy unless she was there with him.

"Are you sure? Because if you're not, we can just forget you ever mentioned it."

He shook his head at her. "Do you like being around me, other than the obvious times?"

"Of course I do. I love being around you." *Careful with your word choice there girl. You don't want him to go running for the hills.*

"Then say you'll move in with me. Come on, what do you have to lose?"

You. She kept the answer to herself. But she answered him anyway. "Okay, I'll move in with you. Just promise me that if you start to get sick of me you'll tell me."

Quinn raised his eyebrows at her. "Get sick of you? Annie, I'm hard for you again already." He kissed her and laughed. "Right. Get sick of you. As if."

Chapter Five

"Wow," Ann said as she sat down across the table from Derek. "I thought you were busy the other night, you guys can't always be this busy. It was crazy in here tonight."

Derek laughed. "It happens every so often. It's like everyone and their mother decides not to cook dinner on the same day."

Ann reached around behind her neck and massaged her tense shoulders. "I could use a hot bath. What time is it anyway?"

Derek held up his hand and squinted at his watch. "Quarter until eleven."

Ann sighed, "Well boss man. If you don't need me anymore, I'm out of here."

Derek made a gesture with his hands for her to head out. He also was tired. "I'm out of here too. Hang on and I'll walk you out."

Ann waited for him by the door and they walked out to the parking lot together. She was getting into her car when he stopped her. "It's later than usual. Maybe I should follow you over to the hotel. You know, just so I can be sure you get home all right. You know with it being Friday night, Quinn will be at the Roadhouse late."

She wasn't sure if they were telling anyone yet. They had only just decided on it that morning. They were going to wait until Sunday to move her things over to his place, because the weekends were always so busy for him at the Roadhouse. But Derek was Quinn's brother so she figured it was okay.

"Actually, I'm not going to the hotel. I took a few of my things over to Quinn's. I'm sort of staying there." She waited for his reaction. He had already given her the brotherly warning. *Would he be okay with this?* They got along really well at work, but she knew that when it came to Quinn, Derek was very protective.

"Staying there? Was there a problem at the hotel?" And he already knew the answer because of the embarrassed way she turned away from him said it all. "Are you two living together now?"

Ann looked back up at him and nodded. "Yeah, I mean he sort of asked me this morning, and I wasn't going to, but I just don't know. It's soon, I know that, I do. There's just something about Quinn, he sort of consumes my mind." She shrugged. "I don't always think rationally when your brother is concerned."

Derek smiled at her. "Nothing you could have said would have mattered more than to me than what you didn't say."

She looked at him perplexed. Sure she knew she was tiptoeing around it, but could she tell him that she was falling for Quinn?

"Derek, I don't understand. All I said was that he sort of clouds my mind." His stare made her feel like he couldn't be happier. He was Quinn's brother, and probably thought that he deserved a good woman. Did he think that she was that one?

His smile only got bigger. "Really? Clouds it huh? Sounds like you got it bad."

Ann smirked at him. He was really very nice, but she knew he was getting a kick out of her discomfort. "Very funny. Fine. I'm crazy about your brother. Is that what you want to hear?"

Derek placed his hands in his front pockets and rocked back and forth on his heels, obviously very pleased with himself. "Yeah, that pretty much covers it. Now come on, I'll follow you to Quinn's. It's late and those dark roads can be pretty dangerous if you're not used to them."

Ann thanked him and closed her door. Starting her engine, she wondered why it was so easy to talk to Derek. Thinking about her past week, she realized just how truly lucky she was. In one week she had found a great job, which she truly enjoyed. She found a sexy and amazing lover! And now she felt like she had an honest to goodness friend in Derek. Suddenly she wasn't angry at Larry anymore. She was actually grateful for his cheating ways. If he had stayed faithful to her, she might not have met Quinn, and she might not have gotten her job or met Derek. *Hmm. Life works in mysterious ways.*

Ten minutes later Ann was getting out of her car. She motioned for Derek to wait before he drove away. She ran over to his window and waited for him to open it.

"You want to come inside?"

He was surprised by her question. She had just told him how exhausted she was. "Ah sure, but I thought you were tired."

She was. Truth was she was beyond tired. But she felt awkward going into Quinn's house. Even though she was going to be living there with him, she still felt like she was intruding upon his personal space. Derek was his brother, so if he came in for a little while then it wouldn't seem so weird.

"I am, but I don't think I'll get to sleep right away anyway. I'm too wound up. We could have a beer or something." She assumed Quinn kept beer at the house. She'd only been over a couple of times before. And then she had just been in the bedroom, although there was that one time in the bathroom, oh and once in the kitchen, too.

"Sure, let me just park my truck. I'll be right inside." Derek watched her as she walked towards the house. She hesitated for a moment before putting her key in the door. Derek picked up his cell phone and called his brother.

"Hey man, what's up?" Quinn asked over the noise surrounding him.

"Nothing major, but we were busy at the restaurant tonight, so we got done much later than usual. Anyway I followed Ann to your place—"

Quinn interrupted him. "Oh, she told you? I was gonna tell you myself, I just got busy."

"No, it's cool. She's nice, I like her, but she seems really nervous. And she asked me to stay. I get the feeling she's afraid to be alone in your place."

Quinn was surprised by his comment. "Really?"

"Yeah, so I'm gonna go inside. But I think she's really exhausted. If you find me sleeping on the sofa when you get home, don't be surprised."

Quinn laughed, "Sure man, thanks for helping her out. She…well she matters…a lot."

Derek grinned as he opened his truck door. "I know. And just so you know, judging from what she told me, the feelings mutual."

"What'd she say?" Quinn was dying to know.

Derek pretended to make static noises and said, "Oh sorry bro, bad connection. Got to go. Bye." And he hung up the phone laughing as he walked to the door.

Quinn hung up his phone and a huge smile formed on his face. She had talked about him to Derek, and it must have been good, otherwise Derek wouldn't have gotten so much enjoyment out of toying with him. He turned his head to look over at the jerk that had been practically molesting Ann on the side of the road last week. He hated the SOB, but suddenly he felt like buying him a beer. If he hadn't been such an arrogant asshole, he might not have pulled over to help her and then he wouldn't be deliriously happy.

Quinn went back out to the main bar area and watched as the usual crowd had too much to drink and got way too rowdy. On any other night he would have been fine with it. But tonight all he could think about was that with every beer sold it was going to be that much longer until he got to go home to be with Ann. He looked around at all the people still crowding the place, knowing that it would be hours before he would get out of there.

* * * *

"So, it looks like we have water or beer." Ann looked up from the refrigerator at Derek, "So, what'll it be?"

"Beer sounds good." He reached his hand over and grabbed onto the frosty bottle. Twisting the top off, he took a long pull on it. "Aah, hits the spot after a long night at the restaurant."

Ann had opted for water and was twisting off her cap, sitting on the breakfast nook stool next to Derek. She sighed before she took a giant swallow. "Yep."

Derek raised an eyebrow at her. He knew she was nervous but now she seemed downright terrified. "What's going on, Ann?"

She looked at him, "I don't know what you mean."

He gave her a mocking half smile, "Yeah, you do. Look I know we haven't known each other that long, but, well we see each other every day and I kind of thought we were becoming friends. I mean you're in love with my brother so—"

"Woah, what did you say? I never…not once did I tell you…I mean I've only known him a week…so I'm not. Alright?" She said matter-of-factly.

Derek wondered if she realized how much she had stammered through her little speech. "Sure. Sorry, I guess I just assumed. You know seeing as how you're, what did you say, 'crazy about him' and for whatever reason you are nervous as all hell to be here. But hey, if you say you don't love him, well then I'll just tell my bro to quit wasting his time on something that's going nowhere," he said it casually as he reached for his cell phone.

Ann's eyes widened in shock, grabbing his phone she stopped him from dialing. "You can't tell him that! What's gotten into you?"

Derek laughed at her, enjoying her little dilemma. "I wasn't really gonna call him. I just wanted to get you to realize that you are falling pretty damn hard for him."

Ann dropped her head on the nook's countertop and groaned. "I know. And because of that it's not going to last."

He bunched his brows together in confusion. "Why is that exactly?"

She made a sound that might have been laughter, he wasn't sure. Then she let out a muffled reply. "Because when I fall for a guy, that's usually around the time he decides that I'm not worth the whole respect and fidelity thing." She raised her head up and looked at Derek. "So you see, no matter how great your brother is now, I give it a couple of weeks before he starts sleeping with other women and treating me like a door mat."

Derek had to bite back his laughter. She clearly didn't see how ridiculous she sounded and how completely torn up she was. "So, now he's great and you are *not* in love with him. But, you are 'crazy about him' which doesn't matter because in a couple of week's time he will become an asshole?"

"Pretty much," Ann said as she reached over and took a healthy swig of his beer.

Derek nodded, "Yeah, that totally makes sense."

Ann knew he was mocking her. "Meaning?"

He just shrugged, "Oh nothing. It's just that my brother hasn't had very much luck with women treating him right. Because of that he's been sort of skittish when it comes to relationships." He took the beer back from her and swallowed some. "Lord knows he's never asked a woman to live with him before. Not to mention insisting that I give one of them a job." He winced at her expression. Obviously she thought that she got the job on merit, which now she would have, because she was a fantastic addition to the restaurant. The customers absolutely adored her. But the real reason he hired her was because Quinn threatened to have some very essential body parts hurt in a very bad way.

"He *made* you hire me?" She should have been more shocked, but she really wasn't. When Quinn wanted something he usually went for it. "Nevermind. It doesn't matter. If you don't want me to stick around, I mean—"

Derek rolled his eyes at her, “Don’t be ridiculous. You’re a great hostess. And unlike our last one, you help out wherever you’re needed. Heck, for all we know, you were the reason for the booming business tonight.”

They both laughed. She really did enjoy talking to Derek. He was almost like the brother she had never had. “Okay. But I am sorry he forced you to hire me. Although it kind of makes sense now, seeing as how the interview consisted of asking my name and to me to fill out a W-4. I like it there though. I hope you know that.”

Swallowing some more of his beer, he nodded. “I do. But enough about the restaurant. Let’s get back to your prince turning into a frog, or in this case, snake theory.”

“Oh no. It’s not a theory. It’s a proven fact. It’s happened to me, more than once, too.” She pointed out.

“That sucks, Ann. Us men can be assholes sometimes. How many men screwed you over?”

“Two.”

Derek was surprised. Quinn told him the other day that she’d only had two boyfriends. He hadn’t said lovers, but it was implied. And to hear that both of those men had hurt her was pretty unbelievable. Especially since she was gorgeous, she had a fantastic personality, and was a lot of fun to be around.

“Only two? That’s hardly enough to base a pattern on. Maybe it’ll be different with Quinn.”

Ann played with the label to her water bottle. “I hope it is. I can’t seem to help myself when I’m with Quinn. I can’t ever say no to him, and why am I telling *you* this?” She got up from the stool in an attempt to hide her embarrassment.

Derek grabbed her wrist and tugged her back to face him. “Because we’re friends. I like you, Ann, and I know Quinn cares about you. You wouldn’t be moving in here if he didn’t. Just don’t overanalyze it okay?”

She slumped back down on the stool. "I know you're right. I just…I mean I liked my other two boyfriends, I even cared about them. But I never felt a connection with them like I do with Quinn." She laughed. "God. Why on earth am I talking to you about your brother? Doesn't that make me weird or something?"

Derek shook his head. "No, it just means you realize a good guy when you see one. Let me be your friend. I care about my brother and I want him to be happy. Just see what happens. Don't worry about what might or could happen. Just enjoy what you have, all right?"

She smiled at him. His pep talk made her feel so much better. She reached over and gave him a hug. "Thank you."

"Sure thing." He patted her on the head teasingly. "Now I'm going to head out of here. Are you going to be a good girl and go to bed?"

She giggled. "Yes, dad."

"Good, come on. Lock the door after I leave."

She walked him to the door and gave him another hug before they both said they'd see each other tomorrow. Ann locked the deadbolt and turned off the front room lights. She walked into the bedroom and began to get ready for bed. Finally, she felt at ease. For some reason Derek's words were able to alleviate the stress she felt at the idea of moving in with Quinn. She knew he was right. She should take things one day at a time. And if she was right and Quinn turned out to be a jerk, then at least she would have had this time with him.

Yeah right. She knew that if Quinn ever hurt her it would be devastating. It wouldn't just make her hurt and angry like Larry had, it would tear her apart. Because try as she might to deny it, she was in love with Quinn Travis.

"God help me," she whispered to herself as she got in bed.

Hours later, Quinn pulled into his driveway. A flutter occurred in his stomach at the sight of Ann's little car sitting in his driveway. Ignoring it, he got out of his truck and headed for the front door. Once inside he headed back to the bedroom and stopped dead in his tracks in the doorway.

Quinn looked at the angel lying in his bed. Because that was the only word to describe her. She was so beautiful. He had thought so from the first moment he saw her. But every time he was inside of her, every time he came and watched in fascination as she came right along with him, it was like her beauty intensified.

Quinn started to undress. Normally, after a long Friday night he would have gotten out of his jeans and t-shirt and went to the kitchen in nothing but his briefs and made himself a sandwich. But now, all he wanted to do was get in bed next to her and hold her.

Sure, he had lain with her many times before. In more ways than one, he thought. But the idea of coming home to her, getting in bed next to her and snuggling her against his body, was sending that warm, fuzzy, fluttery feeling throughout his body. It wasn't even a sexual need now. It was emotional. He just needed to be near her.

Quinn quietly got into bed next to her. He intended to snuggle up against her, but as soon as he was lying down, she rolled over and snuggled against him. *Oh Jesus.* He could feel his heart squeeze with emotion. Damn, he was completely in love with her. One week and he was crazy, head for the hills, out of his mind in love with her.

As he wrapped his arm around her back to hold her closer, he grinned. He was in love. Was he scared? *Sure.* Did he care? *No way!*

Chapter Six

Quinn awoke to the feel of sweet delectable lips brushing against his. He smiled without opening his eyes. He grabbed her quickly and laughed when she squealed in surprise.

"So, you are awake," she said as she trailed a finger down his chest to parts hidden behind black cotton.

He opened one eye and squinted against the bright light. He was definitely not a morning person, but for her he could change that. "I'm awake. Care to see just how awake I am?"

She reached her hand down and cupped his growing erection in her palm. "Hmm. What do we have here, big boy?"

He laughed. Big boy had become her little nick name for him. Despite the seriousness that it implied, it was meant as a joke. Because she reminded him on a daily basis how she was incredibly stupid to turn him away that first time. She explained to him that she must have been suffering from temporary insanity.

"That is yours, Annie." He winked at her and looked confused when she blushed. "What is it?"

She shook her head, "Nothing. It's just that, I really like it when you call me Annie." She shrugged, "It sort of feels like your little nickname for me."

"Oh yeah? Well, tell me. Do you like this?" He brought his mouth to hers and proceeded to kiss her with enough fire to light an entire city aflame.

She didn't answer him, but instead she moaned her response. *God, he's amazing,* she thought.

She tensed underneath Quinn's touch. He pulled back from their kiss. "What's wrong, honey?"

She bit down on her lower lip and shook her head. "Nothing." Leaning over she tried to kiss him again, but he continued to pull back.

"Tell me. I can see you're nervous. I haven't seen that look on your face since the first time we were together. And you know how badly that ended. So tell me what's going on."

She couldn't tell him. How big of a lunatic would she look if she told him that after only one week that she had fallen hopelessly in love with him? So much so, that it was to the point that she was consumed with worry that she might lose him. "I swear it's nothing."

She hoped he didn't know that she was lying. Things were going so good between them. She didn't want to ruin things between them, but she knew moving in with him so soon could be a mistake. One he could live to regret. As if reading her thoughts, he spoke.

"Is this about the living together thing? Because we don't have to, you know? You can stay at the hotel if you want." His words came out quickly as if trying not to rush her.

Great. Was he already changing his mind? It was happening quicker than she thought it would. "Sure. Yeah, you're right. We don't have to rush into anything." She turned away from him and tried to hide the hurt that she felt.

Although her words were killing him, he couldn't ignore the fact that she wouldn't look at him. She was definitely hiding something. He wouldn't rush her, but he wasn't going to lose her to a misunderstanding either. He had to know what was going on inside of her head.

Quinn got up from the bed and went around to the other side. He sat next to her and pulled her up. She still wouldn't look at him, but he turned his body to face hers and used his forefinger to raise her chin. "Look at me, Annie."

She did as he asked. She hated that he saw the way her eyes glistened with tears.

"Baby, what's wrong?" His gut tightened in pain at the sight of her saddened eyes.

She expelled a breath and tried to play it down. She knew she was being silly. They'd only started, well, sleeping together a week ago. She shouldn't be this attached to him already. "It's nothing. I'm sorry."

The look on his face told her that he was angry. Why couldn't she talk to him? What's more was why didn't she think she could trust him?

"That's a lie." He framed her face with his hands and rested his forehead against hers. "Annie, please. Tell me. What's wrong?"

She looked into the depths of his eyes. They were so close to and one another. The gold flecks almost shimmered as she stared at them. They looked so beautiful. The longer she stared into them she became even more convinced than ever that he would leave her. She wished she knew what it was about him that left her feeling so insecure. Even with Larry she knew it was his loss. She knew she was a good catch. But with Quinn she felt like she wasn't enough woman to keep him happy and that pained her more than anything, because she wanted him to be happy. She loved him.

"It's nothing, Quinn. Please let's just forget about it."

He shook his head and kissed her nose. "No," he whispered.

"I can't talk about this. I'm sorry." She got up from the bed and ran into the bathroom and closed the door.

Quinn sat there stunned. *What happened?* In a matter of minutes they went from playful foreplay to her being so upset about something that she was near tears and couldn't look him in the eye. He got up from the bed and went to the bathroom door.

Knocking, he asked her to open it. Which was only met with the sound of the shower turning on. He reached for the handle and was surprised to find it unlocked. He walked in and saw her standing in the shower; she turned to look at him as he came around the door. He wanted to question her. To demand that she tell him what was wrong. But he didn't. He saw the look in her eyes. He knew what she needed. She didn't look as sad as she had only moments before. All he saw in her eyes was desire. Desire for him and what they did to each other.

Quinn stepped out of his briefs and smirked when she licked her lips at the sight of his cock. He fisted it in his hand, stroked it up and down and stepped inside the shower with her. He was going to lean in to kiss her, but suddenly she was on her knees and was swallowing him whole.

"Jesus. Oh god, Annie. Fuck that feels so good." What was she doing? She had gone down on him before. But never with this much zeal. She was acting like she was starving for his cock.

Annie was moaning. She was ravenous for him. As long as she had him she was going to relish every moment of it. Nothing would stand in her way from enjoying him and all of his masculine glory. She moaned again, loving the taste of him, the erotic texture of his smooth skin on his rock hard cock.

Quinn was in heaven and slowly dying for three reasons. First, her wet and hot mouth was performing magic on him. Second, the wet slurping sounds that echoed against the bathroom tiles were so damn erotic he could come from that alone. And third, damn if he didn't love her more and more with every second of every day.

"Oh, Annie. Baby, if you don't stop, I'm gonna come." He gave her the warning but couldn't help himself from pumping into her harder and faster. Hitting the back of her throat over and over again sent him over the edge. "Aahh." He shouted and spurt his hot cum into the deepest parts of her throat.

Ann sucked on him harder. She thrived on the musky and masculine scent and the way he tasted on her tongue. She loved that she had given him such pleasure. Swallowing the last of him, she relaxed her mouth and gently licked the last remaining droplets onto her tongue.

Quinn looked down at her in amazement. His heart clenched once again as she looked up at him. The hot, steamy shower was beating down on them. But he knew that had nothing to do with the flushed look on her face. He gave her a half smile as he brushed his thumb across her jaw line.

"Do you trust me, Annie?"

With everything that I have, she thought. "Yes."

"Good. Come here." He held out his hands to help her up and spun her around. "Place your hands there."

She did as he asked. She leaned the palms of her hands against the small tiled bench in the shower. She could feel him rubbing against her bottom. She closed her eyes and bit back the moan that desperately wanted to escape her mouth. Why did she love it when he did that? Suddenly an image flashed in her mind. An image of Quinn telling her that he wanted to take her there. She felt shocked at her daydream. Why had she imagined such a scenario? She would never do that. She could never. That wasn't normal, was it? She was interrupted from her internal argument by the feel of Quinn reaching over her head.

Quinn grabbed the shower spray and adjusted the nozzle to full massage pressure. Only moments ago, when he thought of it, he just wanted to make her feel as good as she made him feel. But he was already getting hard again. Damn. He wanted her constantly. The sweet and hot wetness of her. The way she clung to and sucked on his cock with her tight pussy. It was amazing.

"Spread your legs a little more baby. Yeah, just like that."

Quinn positioned himself at her entrance, barely sliding inside of her. Nudging just the head of his cock inside. "Are you ready for something new baby?"

Ann's eyes flew open with question. Was he going to–ooh. "Oh Quinn."

Quinn hadn't waited for her answer. Right after he asked her, he slid into her all the way, and at the same time he brought the shower massage nozzle around and in front of her. He sprayed it directly onto her clit as he used the fingers of one hand to open her up further to him. Her resulting response was all the encouragement he needed to thrust into her with so much vigor like he was a virgin on prom night.

Ann could feel her blood beating and coursing through every part of her body and soul. To be filled by him, while he sprayed that fast pounding water against her clit was euphoric. She could already feel her orgasm building. It was right below the surface, climbing up and—ooh. There it is. "Quinn. Yes!" She shouted.

Quinn felt her release wash over his cock as he pumped in and out of her. Knowing that there was no way he was going to be able to come again so soon. But she felt so damn good, he couldn't stop. Annie's words changed his condition really fast, and effectively changed his mind on whether or not he could come again quite so quickly.

"Quinn, please. I want to feel you come inside of me."

Just hearing her he was a goner. He thrust into her twice more and spilled himself inside of her. Surprised that there was anything left, he chuckled at what she did to him. He *was* like a teenage boy. Always hard, and always ready to go.

As they both came down from their orgasms they held onto each other. Not saying anything, they began to wash each other's bodies. When they were drying each other off on the tile floor, Quinn knew that there was no way on God's green earth that he would ever be able to let her go. She was a part of him now. He was a part of her. He hoped to God that she knew that.

* * * *

Ann looked at him and wondered how long she would have with him. Every time they were together she found that she loved him even more. She wished she could tell him, but knew it would just end things sooner. So, she wouldn't say anything. She would just bide her time and hope that she had more time to know him and love him. And dear God, did she love him.

An hour later, Ann followed Quinn into Rose's Diner where they planned to eat a late breakfast. There was no mistaking all of the heads that turned in their direction as they entered.

"Just how small is this town?" She asked him as they sat down.

He chuckled. "Only a little over a thousand. Didn't you know that? Why did you move here anyway?"

"I guess I needed a change of scenery."

He smiled at her and outstretched his arms across the back of the booth. "And? What do you think of the scenery so far?"

She laughed at his arrogance. "Me like."

"You do huh? Well, I happen to be enjoying the scenery as well." He reached over and laced their fingers together.

"Seriously though, over a thousand people? That doesn't seem terribly small. It seems like everyone knows everyone, and their business," she added at the end.

"Not really. It's just that everyone has known each other for so long and sees one another so often it's kind of hard to keep secrets around here." He shrugged it off, used to everyone's nosiness.

"Oh, so basically the idea of privacy is foreign in this town?"

He gave her an 'oh please' grin. "No. But everyone knew my parents and their sordid situation, so naturally they know me and Derek, too." He had already told her about his parents, after she had mentioned to him what Derek had said.

"Well, I happen to think you're a very major player, at least in my life anyway."

He knew she was only being playful, but he needed to hear that. He needed to know that he was important to her. He wished he could tell her everything that was happening to him. Everything that he felt at even the thought of her. But he had to be careful, he had to make sure he didn't rush her. He could be patient. When she was ready, and she felt just as strongly for him too, then he would tell her.

Ann looked at him sitting across the booth. It still amazed her how incredibly handsome he was. After this morning, she managed to fall even farther over the edge in love with him. She actually had to bite her tongue from screaming it when she came in the shower earlier. She knew that she would have to wait until either he felt the same way towards her too, or he got tired of her and moved on. Regardless of which way it went she knew she would someday tell him everything that he was to her.

Chapter Seven

"Do you realize that it's been two weeks since you seduced me on the side of the road?" Quinn asked her over a plate of scrambled eggs.

Ann looked at him innocently and held a hand to her chest in shock. "What? Me? Seduce you? I am a lady, sir, whatever gave you the impression that I would stoop to such levels?"

Quinn almost spit out his eggs in laughter. "Well you may not stoop but you certainly drop, to your knees, a lot."

Ann gasped at his cocky arrogance. She picked up her napkin and threw it at him. "Well, you are certainly never complaining when I'm doing it."

After he dodged her napkin he explained, "No, you misunderstood. I'm not complaining. No, I'm merely pointing out how glad I am that you had that flat tire." He winked at her and shoveled in another forkful of eggs.

"Fine. I guess you're saved by your charm. So, what's on the agenda today?"

He thought about it for a minute. This was the first day since they met that they both actually had the day off. It was strange and nice feeling being able to sleep late without either one of them needing to be anywhere.

"No ideas, huh?" Ann reached over and grabbed his empty plate in an effort to take it to the sink. But her idea was quickly thwarted.

Quinn pulled her into his lap. "I have a few ideas." He waggled his brows at her in a seductive gesture.

Ann rolled her eyes and laughed at him. "Good Lord. Don't you ever get enough?" But she kissed him anyway. She loved his kisses and the drugging effect they had on her senses.

Quinn was the first to pull away. He looked at her intently as he ran a hand up her arm, across her shoulder and up her neck to cup her nape. "I don't. I swear, no matter how many times we're together I'm always dying for you again."

Ann seemed startled by his demeanor. She said nothing, rather staring at him.

"Annie, say something." Quinn's words came out desperate, and he hated that. But he needed something from her. He needed a sign that he was as important to her as she was to him. So many times in the past week he had almost let it slip that he was in love with her. He just kept reminding himself that they had only been together for two weeks. That he had to be patient and soon, hopefully, she would fall in love with him, too.

"Quinn, I don't know what to say when you get serious like that." Her expression showed him how sincere she was being. She still looked unsure, as if afraid to tell him the whole truth. He wished the woman in her would scream from the highest mountain top that she loved him. It was too soon for that though and he knew it. He hated this tightening feeling around his heart. He wanted to keep her forever and feared that he might not be able to.

"You could tell me that you feel the same way. You could tell me that you want me just as much as I want you." It wasn't really all that he needed to hear, but it was a beginning.

As soon as he said it he realized his mistake. Sex again. Would that be her biggest worry? Would she wonder if all he was interested in was the way their bodies moved so in tune with one another? Sure, it was fantastic. Heck, it was better than fantastic, but he wanted more for them.

She set the plate back on the table and reached her arms around his neck. "I do want you, Quinn. You know that though. It's obvious isn't it? Every time you touch me I completely melt for you." *How could he not know that?* She was a whimpering pile of need for him.

He smiled at her and kissed her nose. He did know that. He knew how to turn her on and make her feel good. Of that he was sure. But he wanted more than her body. He wanted her to give her heart, willingly and without reservations. He wanted all of her, every last bit of her, right down to her very soul. Hell, he didn't just want that, he needed it.

"Do you feel like taking a drive today?" He asked her as he continued to plant little kisses all along her face. "We could take a picnic up to a lake that's only about an hour away. Maybe a blanket, too? What do you say?"

It sounds like heaven. "I think that sounds great. Do you want me to make some sandwiches? I could even throw a salad together."

He didn't. One of the things he had noticed since she moved in was that she was always trying to do things for him. This would have been nice occasionally, but she did it like she was trying to prove something to him. She did the dishes, the laundry, cleaned, dusted and vacuumed. They actually had had their first argument over it a couple of days ago.

He remembered vividly the hurt in her eyes when he had snapped at her. He hadn't meant to, but he had just gotten home late from the Roadhouse and was furious when he found her still up at three o'clock in the morning folding his laundry.

"Why in the hell are you doing the wash at this ungodly hour?" He had snapped at her.

At first she had snapped back. "I didn't get home until late from the restaurant and I knew if I didn't do it that you'd try to do it yourself tomorrow."

It baffled him why she kept trying to do things before he got to them. He couldn't make any sense out of it. "Why? So what if I do the laundry. It's my laundry."

That was when she changed, when the sadness entered her eyes. "I just want to do nice things for you. I didn't want you to think that I don't appreciate you letting me stay here."

In retrospect he could have handled her statement better. The truth was though that it pissed him off. He wasn't just letting her stay there. He had asked her to move in with him and he meant it. He didn't want her 'staying' with him. He wanted her living with him. It was supposed to be their place, together. Not her staying with him. It made it sound like they were just biding their time until something better came along.

So naturally, because he was so levelheaded whenever he got angry, he really flew off the handle. "I don't want you to fucking appreciate it. I want you to enjoy it, damn it. I want you to stop thinking that you have to do things for me to make me happy."

But his harsh words and the way he screamed brought tears to her eyes, and that was something that he couldn't handle. He instantly apologized, and held her close as he told her how sorry he was. She sniffled a little before accepting it, but it still tore through his heart to hear her cry, especially since he was the one that had caused it.

And the real kicker to the whole thing was that while he was battling her in her constant efforts to do nice things for him, he was dying to do the same. He wanted to be the one to do the nice things, to take care of her and sweep her off of her feet until she fell hopelessly in love with him.

"No, don't make anything. We'll pick up some fried chicken on the way. Let's not worry about anything today and just relax." He held her a little tighter and closer to her body. "Let's go get ready okay?" And he swiftly patted her butt as she stood up.

"You go ahead. I want to get these dishes done before we leave." She wasn't looking at him; she was already soaping up the sponge and preparing to wash the pan that she had made the eggs in.

He wanted to tell her no. That she wasn't going to do the dishes and she was going to come to the shower with him right now. But he didn't. There was no way that he was going to do anything to ruin their day together. So instead he left the room and headed toward the bedroom. He wished he could make her get over the need to take care of him and do things for him. But he wouldn't force the issue today. Today, they would just enjoy themselves. They would be able to stay all day if they wanted. His assistant manager was covering for him at the Roadhouse tonight, and there was nothing standing in their way of just simply enjoying each other.

Two and a half hours later Quinn pulled up alongside the lake. He watched her reaction as she took in her surroundings. "What do you think?"

She looked over at him and smiled. "It's breathtaking. How did you ever find it?"

Quinn shrugged as he put the truck in park. "Our dad used to take Derek and I here when we were kids. We would stand over there on the shore and fish for hours." He laughed a little as he remembered those days. "It's weird you know, he was a horrible, rotten husband. Geez, he was as absolute asshole to our mothers, with the way he constantly broke both of their hearts with empty promises, but he was such a good dad."

Ann reached over and touched his arm. She needed to give him comfort. He was clearly not only remembering his father but missing him as well.

Quinn placed his hand over hers. "It's a strange contradiction. In some ways he was a great person, but in others ways he just sucked."

"Quinn, I don't mean to appear insensitive. But you've told me, and so has Derek, that both of your mothers knew. That they both knew and loved him anyway." She stared back at him when he turned towards her. "I'm not saying what he did was right, but it seems like they sort of enabled him to treat them that way. He knew neither one of them would turn him away. Maybe that's why he kept doing it."

Quinn was surprised at how well she had summed up the numerous conversations him and Derek had had in the past.

Everything she said was true, he knew that. But deep down Derek and Quinn had always hoped that he would just choose one of them and stop hurting the other, instead of hurting both of them, all the time.

She looked away nervously. Why had she said that? She should have kept her opinion to herself. “I’m sorry, that probably sounded cold and unfeeling.”

“Not at all, honey. I was just thinking how right you were.” He lifted his hand and brushed his fingers against her cheek. “Come on. Let’s go have our picnic.”

Minutes later they had the blanket laid out and then Quinn had sat down and leaned up against a tree trunk. He motioned for her to join him, and she did, happily. She sat down in between his legs and leaned into the warmth of his solid chest. He wrapped his arms around her and kissed the top of her head.

“Are you hungry? Because I’m not.” She told him as she leaned further into his embrace, loving the way that it felt to be wrapped up in his arms.

“No, I’m not hungry. Let’s just sit here, I want to hold you honey.” He all but whispered the words, he was so quiet.

Ann loved it when he would become so attentive and treat her with such tenderness. She wished she didn’t have these underlying insecurities. Quinn was wonderful to her. It was silly to worry that she might lose him. And yet that was still her greatest fear. Neither Larry nor Brett were half the man that Quinn was. She knew she shouldn’t hold him accountable for how they treated her.

She tried to erase the anxiety from her mind. She wanted to enjoy being here with him in such a beautiful place. That’s what she was concentrating on when she fell asleep.

Quinn was talking for a minute or so when he realized that she wasn’t listening intently to every word that he said because she was sleeping. He rested his head against the side of hers and breathed in her scent. She always smelled so feminine and pretty.

So Quinn sat and held her, listening to her even breathing. She even breathed beautifully. How any one woman could be so amazing completely fathomed him. He was becoming utterly consumed by her. In such a short time, she had become the most important person in the entire world. Hell, she was his world.

Close to an hour later, Quinn felt her stirring in his arms. He had to admit that he was getting stiff from holding her so still for so long. But a part of him was disappointed that she was waking up.

Ann blinked as she opened her eyes. Had she fallen asleep? And where was—oh, he was still here holding her. She looked over her shoulder up at him.

Quinn gave her a huge grin and winked at her. "Sleep well, honey?"

She sighed at his sweetness. "Yes, how long was I sleeping for?"

He shrugged and kissed her on her forehead. "Almost an hour."

Ann shook her head. "You should have woken me. You didn't have to hold me the whole time. Gosh, Quinn, you must be so sore."

He was, but not just his arms. He had been aching in a different way for her for at least half of the time she was asleep. Because the feel of her soft round bottom pressed firmly against him almost drove him insane. Somehow he was going to have to get this fantasy of his in check. He knew there was no way that Ann would ever want to. It was amazing she was able to handle him at all. The sheer idea that she would be able to take him into her body there didn't seem realistic. But oh Lord, how he wanted to. . He wanted to sink into her tiny whole and fill her with himself.

"Yoo hoo, Quinn?" She laughed. "Where'd you go?"

"Nowhere, honey. I'm right here." And he kissed her. He kissed her long and hard until she was just as urgent for him. He might not get his fantasy, but he had her. And he wouldn't take that for granted.

Quinn laid her down on the blanket and unbuttoned the top of the pretty yellow and white sundress she was wearing. He loved how her pale skin seemed almost tan against the light pastel of the dress. Once he had the buttons undone down to her waist he used his hands to pull the two sides of the dress open, exposing her to him.

"Lord, honey. I never get used to how beautiful you are."

Ann loved when he talked to her like that. Like she truly was the most beautiful woman he had ever seen. "I want you, Quinn."

Quinn loved when she talked to him like that. Like he was the most amazing lover in the entire world. "I want you too, babe. But not yet. I want to kiss every inch of you."

Ann's skin heated at his words. And just like before, she could feel and hear her skin sizzling with every gentle glide of his tongue.

Quinn leaned over her and hungrily grabbed onto a nipple with his mouth. Suckling on it, he laved it with his tongue and gently bit down with his teeth. She was so responsive to his touches that he couldn't help himself from exploring more of her. He reached his hands under her dress and yanked her panties down. Lifting her dress completely and bunching it up at her waist, Quinn kissed her where he really wanted to.

Ann moaned and arched into him as he kissed her passionately at the apex of her thighs. Her body was humming and her pussy was throbbing with need for him. The feel of his tongue laving around her throbbing lips was causing a heat to course through her veins and shoot straight down to her aching sex. She had to have him inside of her. She would surely die if she couldn't hold him to her body while he was buried deep inside of her. Her saturated folds were clinging and sucking on him as he thrust into her.

"Quinn, please I can't wait anymore."

He chuckled at her urgent request. He loved driving her crazy. "Soon, babe. Just relax, let me please you."

"Quinn if you don't stop soon I'm—" Too late. Ann just smiled and screamed his name when the orgasm swept through her body.

He lapped up every drop that poured from her. He continued to feast on her, ravenous for more of her sweetness, until he also could take no more. Quinn sat up and unbuttoned his jeans. Gazing into her eyes he slid his zipper down and pulled his pants down to his knees.

"Now, honey."

Ann stretched her arms out to him as she spread her legs further apart to welcome him into her. "Now. Take me Quinn. Do it like you do when you can't get enough of me."

No problem there, he thought to himself. He smiled at her as he positioned himself and took her, sliding into the liquid heat of her. "Oh fuck, babe. Damn, I can't get enough of you."

Ann almost cried at his words. Sure they weren't the prettiest, but they were his and they surmised everything that she felt. Because she couldn't get enough of him either.

"Are you ready, honey?"

She smiled, knowing exactly what he meant. He always started off slow, but then he would lose control and fuck her with such zeal she would swear that he needed it just as much as he needed air. She nodded because she loved when this part came.

Quinn pounded into her, hard and fast. He could hear his balls hitting against the back of her ass. Oh sweet Jesus, her ass. He wanted to take her there so badly. He wanted to spread a slippery lubricant all over her tiny hole and sink way deep down inside of her. Damn, he had to stop thinking about this. It was never going to happen.

"Annie, I'm already so close. Touch yourself honey. Rub your clit for me." When she didn't do what he asked, Quinn took her hand and guided it down to meet with her soaking pussy.

"Mmm." She moaned her approval.

"That's my girl, yeah baby. Rub it. Make yourself come. Oh Jesus babe." Quinn was like a caged animal suddenly free for the very first time. Watching her touch herself, and thinking about what he wanted to do to her sent him over the edge.

"I'm gonna come, honey."

Ann got there first and lost herself in her second orgasm in mere minutes. The convulsing muscles of her pussy sucked and stroked his cock and sent Quinn over into oblivion to join her. He flung his head back and shouted her name as his hot seed squirted deep inside of her.

This was absolute utopia, Quinn thought. She had better fall in love with him soon because he was dying to tell her everything that she meant to him.

Chapter Eight

Ann had just finished bussing a table when Derek came up behind her and startled her.

"What are you doing?" He asked her with anger in his voice.

After she calmed her racing pulse she picked up the tray of dishes and headed back to the kitchen. All the while rolling her eyes because she knew what he was upset about and she really didn't feel like rehashing it again. The argument was getting old.

"Ann, answer me." He stormed into the kitchen behind her.

Luckily, the restaurant was empty with customers but the kitchen staff stood there wide eyed as they watched their boss yell at her. A custom that they were not used to seeing from him.

After setting the tray of dishes down next to the dishwashing station she turned to him. Placing her hands on her hips she took a deep breath and sighed. "Derek, why do we always have to fight about this?"

This time Derek placed his hands on his hips. "Oh, I don't know, maybe it's because I'm the boss and you are my employee and you *never* do as I tell you."

That made her laugh. Derek really wasn't the assertive type. He was in fact the exact opposite of Quinn. It was one of the reasons it was so easy to talk to him. But listening to him now as he tried to take charge was more than a little funny.

"This isn't funny, Ann. I told you to go home. You've been here for ten hours." He pointed out to her.

Ann expelled a large breath and looked at the kitchen staff who she knew also thought she was insane. "Derek, please. You know I hate going home and sitting there while Quinn is still at the Roadhouse. I'm too wound up after work and I just end up sitting there and staring at the walls."

He was about to say something, but she quickly cut him off. "And besides, you needed the extra help tonight, what with Claire being out with the flu and all. So, rather than yelling at me you should be thanking me."

Derek hated when she applied reason to their arguments. "Maybe I did need your help but that doesn't change the fact that you were insubordinate and I could fire you for that alone."

That statement brought the entire kitchen to hysterical laughter. He was the most easy going boss there was. He never yelled, wasn't demanding, didn't expect unreasonable results and treated everyone like they were more family then employee.

"Ha ha very funny." Derek told everyone in the kitchen. "I could fire her right now if I wanted to."

"But you wouldn't, boss." Leo their head cook told him.

"Wouldn't? Heck, he couldn't, he's too damn nice. That's the only reason we were stuck with that other god awful hostess for so long. If she hadn't quit we'd still be stuck with her and we wouldn't have Ann here." This was from Frances, one of their waitresses.

Derek looked at Ann and turned about six shades of pink. He had told Ann that he had fired the girl. He hadn't meant to lie to her, but after he had gone on and on about how horrible she was, she had said, 'so naturally you fired her' to which he responded 'of course.' Because what was he going to say? That he was just too nice to do it and he always thought that everyone deserved the benefit of the doubt and a second chance?

"I thought you fired her." Ann said.

This only made the staff laugh louder.

"Fine. You think I'm too nice? Well how about this, you're all fired!" Derek stormed out of the kitchen and left the door swinging back and forth.

Ann stared at the door, feeling horrible for the embarrassment she saw on Derek's face. "You guys, it's not funny. He looked really upset."

"Just wait," Leo said.

"Yeah," said Frances. "I'd give it about ten, no make that five, four, three, two, one and here he comes."

Ann looked at Frances dumbfounded when she saw Derek walk back into the room at the exact moment she had predicted.

"I'm sorry, guys. I didn't mean that. Of course you're not all fired. Please accept my apologies." When Derek left again, he didn't storm or stomp, he just calmly walked out of the room.

Ann looked to Frances when he left. "What was that about?"

Frances just shrugged. "Sometimes we tease him too much. Every so often he gets a little fired up and threatens to fire us all. He always comes right back and apologizes."

"That's horrible," Ann told them.

"Yeah," Frances said. "We actually panicked the first couple of times thinking that he really meant it, but we soon learned it's his way of standing his ground. He must have inherited his mother's non-confrontational behavior, because he's nothing like your Quinn."

Her Quinn. She liked the sound of that. "Well, I think it's mean and you guys should apologize for laughing at him."

Leo shook his head. "He would never let us. We've tried a few times. It just hurts his pride. It has more to do with Sandi than it does with anything else. Ouch, what'd you hit me for?" He asked Frances.

"That's not our business to tell." She told him.

"Who's Sandi?"

"No one." Frances answered. "Come on let's get finished so we can get out of here."

A little over an hour later Ann watched everyone walk out the back door of the restaurant. She usually walked out with Derek so she saw no reason to make tonight any different. Hesitantly, she walked back to Derek's office. After his little outburst in the kitchen, he went in there and shut the door, not opening it once, which wouldn't have been that big of a deal if he didn't make a habit of helping the staff clean up each and every night. She knocked on the door and waited for him to answer.

"Come in." Derek's voice was quiet and barely recognizable.

Ann was ready to greet him with a friendly smile, but then she saw the condition he was in. "Derek? Are you…okay?"

Derek looked up at her and laughed. "I'm great, baby. You?"

Baby? Oh Lord. "How much have you had to drink?" Although it was a stupid question. She knew that bottle of Jack Daniels had been completely full only hours ago.

"Oh, not much, just a teensy weensy bit." He motioned for her to sit down and join him. "Here. Take a load off." Without even asking her if she wanted any, he put a shot glass in her hand.

"Derek, I'm not much of a drinker."

"Now Ann, you already embarrassed me in front of everyone. At least do me the honor of having a drink with a pretty lady." He winked at her and slammed another shot.

Pretty lady? He was obviously drunker than she thought, because he was downright flirting with her and that was something that he never ever did.

"Derek, I think that maybe you should let me drive you home. You know, so you can sleep it off."

Derek cocked a brow up and looked at her. "Are you trying to take advantage of me? Because I have to say, you don't need to take advantage, I'd be a willing participant."

Now that pissed her off. They had become good friends, and now he was going to say something stupid like that and try to ruin things? Well, she wasn't going to let him.

"Derek, that's enough." She slammed her shot glass on his desk causing it to spill over the rim.

"Oh, now what'd you go and do that for? You just wasted some perfectly good whiskey." Proving his seriousness he picked up her glass and licked the side of it before swallowing its contents.

"Damn it, Derek! Why are you acting this way? What has gotten into you?"

Derek just grinned at her and waggled his brows. "What about you, huh? What's gotten into you? How about me? You want me to get into you?"

Whap! Ann couldn't help it, she was angry with him for his blatant remarks. He knew how she felt about Quinn and this wasn't him. Derek didn't act like this. He didn't hit on her. He had too much love and respect for his brother. She knew it was the alcohol talking, but it didn't stop her from being mad enough to strike him.

"Shit! What the hell did you do that for?" Derek was rubbing his jaw and wincing.

"I did that," she reached over and grabbed the bottle from him. "Because you're being an asshole."

Derek looked at her for a moment before he responded to her accusation. "I'm sorry." He sank in his chair and rested his head in his hands.

Derek shook his head from side to side. "Derek, what's wrong? What happened in the kitchen earlier. You know they were just teasing you, right? They didn't mean to upset you."

His head was still hanging down. "I know. I do, it's just that whenever I get accused of being too nice it pisses me off." He jerked his head up and looked at her. "I mean, what the hell is wrong with being a nice guy? I can think of worse damn things to be. And so what if I'm nice. It's not like I treat people like shit. That should be a good quality, instead it's like a freaking cross I have to bear."

Ann listened to him vent. She wondered if his pain had anything to do with the girl, Sandi, that Frances and Leo had mentioned. She weighed her options on whether or not she should bring her up. But

Derek had been so good to her. He had become a true friend to her. Maybe she could be the same for him.

"Derek, is this about Sandi?"

A tornado couldn't whip around as fast as his head did at her question. "Who told you about Sandi?"

"No one, really. I just sort of overheard Frances and Leo saying that, well, maybe whatever happened with her has to do with why you get so sensitive about the whole being nice thing." She shouldn't have ratted out Frances and Leo, but the only thing she was worried about right now was Derek.

"They talk about me? About that? Oh great. I'm not pathetic enough right. Jesus!" Derek flung himself in his chair for the second time.

"It's not what you think. They like you and care about you. I think they're actually worried about you."

Derek didn't look at her or say anything. He just motioned with his hands for her to sit in the chair across from him.

Ann sat down and waited for him to break the silence. She had a feeling he just needed time before he said whatever was consuming his thoughts at that moment.

"We were engaged."

That was all he said, just three little words. But the pain that she heard in his voice spoke volumes of what those words meant. Clearly he had been hurt.

"What happened?"

"I still don't know. I swear it's so freaking confusing. It's been a year and I still can't forget it." He didn't say what he really wanted to, and that was that after one year he still wasn't over it, or over her. He still loved her.

"Do you want to talk about it?"

He laughed, an agonized sound. "What's there to talk about? I can't make heads or tails of what went wrong. All I know is one night changed our lives forever. And the Sandi that I knew and loved was gone."

Okay, so that made absolutely no sense. "Derek, I'm not saying you have to talk about it. But if you feel like it, I'm here, and I'm a good listener."

He looked at her as he leaned back in his chair and crossed his arms over his chest. Apparently he was deciding whether or not to talk about it because she could see him pondering what to do. He rocked back in his chair a couple of times before he finally said something.

"I met her about five years ago. She was the Gallagher's niece. Remember, they were here last…Tuesday. The guy with the funny-looking toupee. Anyway, she had come out to visit one summer with her family. She just turned twenty, still so young and sweet, naïve I guess you could say. Anyway, I met her at the Roadhouse. I was helping Quinn out. His door guy called in sick, so I was working for him. It was Friday night and busy as all hell. I was so busy checking ID's that I barely noticed her. I glanced at her ID and was all set to let her go inside, but when I handed it back to her our fingers touched and," he rolled his eyes, "this is gonna sound really corny, but there was like a spark between us. At that one moment when our fingers touched, I felt like I had been electrocuted, but in a good way. You know?"

Boy did she. Being with Quinn was like constant overload to her senses. She knew exactly what it meant to feel your skin heat and sizzle with desire and urgent need for someone. But instead of telling him all of that, she just nodded in agreement.

"Anyway, that's when I really looked at her." He started to laugh. "The little sneak had stolen her sister's ID, which granted they did look a lot alike, but I could tell they weren't the same person. Of course I told her she couldn't go in, and I took her sister's ID, told her that her sister would have to come pick it up."

Derek shrugged, "It's policy. We can't very well give her back the ID she's trying to use to get into bars. So, I guess I sort of embarrassed her, what with me doing it in front of all the people that were crowded around outside. She decided to wait around until I left that night. She was that pissed. She waited for over six hours until I came stumbling out to my truck, dead tired from a long day."

He expelled a huge breath before continuing, "I get out there, start to unlock my door and I feel someone slapping me in the back, not just a little slap either. More like the kind when two girls are really going at it, you know like in a cat fight. I mean she wasn't using her fists, but they sure felt like punches. I turned around to see what in the hell was happening, because that's what I thought, I was like what the hell? Anyway, I see this pretty little blonde-haired blue-eyed princess glaring at me, but behind that glare I could tell that she had been crying. I gotta tell you, it about broke my heart to see tears in those pretty little eyes."

Ann was on the edge of her seat with his story, waiting anxiously to hear what happened next. She had to ask him to continue because for a moment he got lost in the memories.

"Sorry. I should have cursed, yelled or something, because damn, her slaps really hurt. Instead I grabbed her and held her close. And before you even ask, I have no freaking idea why I did it. It was the strangest thing. She was beating the crap out of me. For all I knew, she was a little delinquent, because, you know, she was trying to sneak in bars and all. But her tears, oh God, her tears were like a knife cutting through my heart. I just had an overwhelming feeling to hold her and comfort her. And the funny thing is, she didn't push me away. She just held onto me and cried."

"So why was she so upset? I mean you embarrassed her, but to be that upset? Isn't that a bit extreme?"

"Yeah, I guess. I mean, apparently there were a group of local kids that she had met earlier that day at the Stop-N-Go. She didn't have any friends in town, and she was going to be here for three months, so she tried to become their friend. Only these kids just wanted to mess with her. They knew she was underage, and they also knew there was no way that she'd get into the Roadhouse. So, they told her that if she wanted to hang out with them, she had to find a way to get in. But, rather than me let her in, I took her ID, made some sort of comment about her being a little girl, and sent her on her way. I guess they razzed her pretty bad. So yeah, it might seem extreme to get that upset. But at the time I understood. I mean she was still so young, she had no friends and absolutely no one to talk to. By the way, I neglected to mention that her parents had the personality of a wet mop and pretty much treated her like she was a nuisance. So, she needed a friend and I took away her only hope of making any."

Ann listened to Derek and tried to put herself in the girl's shoes. Maybe it might have been a little humiliating, she thought. "So, then what happened?

"It took some doing, but I calmed her down a little bit and we talked. We both sat on the tailgate of my truck, and we talked until the sun came up. It was actually kind of nice. I'd never stayed out with a girl all night before and just talked. Somehow in the hours that passed, I ended up holding her hand. I'm not really sure who had initiated it, but it was nice. I followed her home, expecting to have to deal with her father. You know, your twenty year old daughter is out all night and she comes home in the morning with an older guy following her. I guess I figured there'd be hell to pay. But nothing even remotely close to that happened. Her parents were just coming out of the house when we pulled up. They just looked at her and told her that they hadn't realized she wasn't home. Then they said that she would have to find herself something to eat because they were going out to get something. Then they just left. No worries or concern over where she was, or the strange man that was with her. It was kind of sad."

"And embarrassing. Seeing as how you were there to witness it," Ann added.

"Yeah, it was. I could see it on her face, too. Only being with her a few hours and I could tell just by looking at her what she was feeling. So, I considered my options. One, I could say goodbye and leave. Or two, I could get out of my truck and give her a hug and ask her to breakfast."

"Well, what'd you decide?"

Quinn just gave her a 'oh please' look. "What do you think that I did?"

She grinned. In the short time that she knew, Derek he was gallant if nothing else. He didn't like it when women were upset about anything. "You took her to breakfast."

He nodded. "I did. I took her to breakfast and afterwards, when I brought her home, I kissed her. It wasn't sexual or passionate. It was just a simple little kiss. But I got to tell you, that little kiss packed one hell of a punch. Because at that very moment I was hooked. She was just so damn sweet. So pretty, she was every fantasy a man has when he pictures his future wife."

Ann raised her eyebrows at that. "You knew that day that you wanted to marry her?"

"Hell yeah I did. She was amazing. I'm not saying that I actually fell in love with her then. But I was pretty damn close. Sort of like teetering on the edge, so to speak. Anyway, we spent the next several weeks dating. You know, getting to know each other. It was different with her. Every other woman I had dated I was sleeping with by the second date. But Sandi was different. And it was more than a little obvious that she was a virgin. I didn't want to rush her. Lord knows we had plenty of opportunities. She stayed at my house all the time. Her parents never cared where she was. But, I usually just ended up holding her and cuddling with her."

Derek laughed. "It's kind of funny when you think about it. I mean, I slept with her before I ever slept with her. Sorry, bad joke. Anyway, one day I came home from work and she was already at my place. She had candles and flowers everywhere, not that I needed them of course, but she did. She went to great lengths to make sure that her first time, our first time together, was perfect. And it was, you know. It was more than perfect. If I hadn't already been in love with her then, that night sealed the deal. I was hers, completely, from that moment on."

Ann closed her eyes and tried to hide the emotions swirling inside of her. While her and Quinn's first time together hadn't been romantic with flowers and candles, there was still something deep inside that happened to her, making her feel so at peace and content. So she knew exactly what Derek meant when he said it was perfect.

"So, to speed things up a bit to my devastating heartbreak, we moved in together, did everything together. We were absolutely inseparable, and it wasn't a bad thing. It was great actually. She got a job working at that hotel you were staying at and she was happy. We were happy. Until a little over a year ago. Then everything changed."

Ann reached her hand across the desk to take Derek's in hers. The happiness that was in his eyes only minutes ago had vanished. He was upset again and hurting. "You don't have to tell me if you don't want to."

Derek squeezed her hand and shook his head. "No. It's good for me to talk about it. And truth be told, you're easy to talk to. You don't mind hearing it?"

"No, I'm honored that you would trust me enough to talk about it with me."

"Okay, her sister, you know the one whose ID she had stolen? She was getting married. We were both going, but the weekend before the wedding, she flew to Denver for the bachelorette party. It was no big deal. I loved her and trusted her. We actually just got engaged about a month before, so I had no reason to think that I should be worried. But I was wrong."

Ann waited. Whatever he was about to tell her was killing him. She could see the pain reflected in his eyes.

Derek looked up at her and then away. “They went to an All Male Revue. I mean, I knew she was going. I didn’t care, heck I’d gone to bachelor parties that had ended up in strip clubs so I didn’t see anything wrong with it. But apparently this one guy, a dancer was hitting on her pretty bad. She did the right thing. Told him she was engaged and that she was taken. So I should have been happy, right?”

“Right. Why do I get the impression that you weren’t, though?”

“When I got out there to the wedding I overheard some of the bridesmaids talking at the reception. Talking about how this guy had been hounding her all week. Apparently, Sandi had met him a couple of times for drinks. Oh damn, was I pissed. I confronted her later that night at the hotel. She admitted to meeting him twice. But she swore that nothing happened. She swore that she only went there to insist that he leave her alone. She claimed she told him that she was engaged and she wasn’t free to see other men.”

Ann wondered if he realized what he’d said.

“I know, that’s what I thought, too. Not once while she was telling me how innocent their meetings were did she tell me that she didn’t want to see him. She kept saying that she was already taken, so she wasn’t *free* to see him. Like I was standing in her way or something. Needless to say, I was pissed off.”

Ann started to speak, but he quickly cut her off.

“No, wait for it, it gets better. So, we have a huge fight and I fly back home by myself. A week later she comes crawling back to me. Saying that she’s sorry and that I’m what she really wants. Not him. I should have been ecstatic, but I knew there was something she wasn’t telling me. And I also knew that she could never look me in the face and lie to me. So I asked her what it was, and I got to tell you a part of me wishes I hadn’t. Because at that moment my heart literally stopped beating. I stood there and listened while she told me she slept with him.”

“Oh, Derek. I’m so sorry.”

He shook his head. “Don’t be. She’s the one that did it. I, being the dumbass that I am, was willing to give her another chance. And despite the fact that I was angry, jealous and pissed off as all hell, things were going okay for about a month. But I could sense something was off. She changed, if only a little, but I could tell. I told myself it was just guilt that she was feeling. But when I came home one day I learned just how stupid that was.”

Derek’s eyes welled up with tears. He couldn’t fight the emotions that overcame him with the memory of that day. “I walked in my house, expecting to sit down to dinner with her. I guess I was earlier than usual or she had lost track of time, because the second I walked in the house I heard them.”

Derek ran his fingers through his hair and groaned in frustration. “I planned to just walk down the hall and walk in on them, if nothing else then for the pure satisfaction of seeing the look on her face when I caught her. But I stopped right outside the door. She was screaming, shouting really, telling him to fuck her harder, fuck her like she loves it, like Derek couldn’t. She actually said those words. That I couldn’t fuck her like she wanted. I heard a slap, peeked in the door and saw that she was getting spanked with a flogger.”

Derek saw the confused look on her face. “It’s like a small rubber whip. Fuck, Ann. You have no idea what it felt like to know that not only she had gone to another man, but that she didn’t think I could do those things for her.”

Derek saw that she was once again confused. “See I have a bit of an unusual appetite when it comes to my sexual preferences. But with her, I always held back. I guess I thought she was too special to subject her to any of my deepest, darkest desires. And I can see from the look on your face that I’ve made you uncomfortable.”

“No. No, I’m just surprised. So, if she, um, needed that and you wanted it too, why couldn’t you work things out?”

“Because I didn’t go in right away. I stayed outside the room and listened and watched. I don’t know why, but I felt like I had to. And unfortunately, I'm glad that I did. Because she kept talking. She kept telling him things, intimate things about us. She told him how I was too nice to her, how she wanted me to force her to do things like he did. She also told him that it never felt as good as it did when he was fucking her. That was the last straw; I stormed in the bedroom and kicked the asshole out of our house."

"That must have been horrible for you," Ann told him sincerely.

"It was. It was the worst pain I'd ever felt in my life. She actually turned to someone else because she thought I was too good to her. I mean shit, Ann. I fucking loved her so much I thought I would die from it. I never wanted to subject her to the kind of kinky things I was into. Sorry. I don't know what else to call it."

"That's okay. What would you call it?" Why she asked, she had no idea. But curiosity had gotten the better of her. Because despite the pain of his story, she couldn't help but feel some sort of connection to it. She herself was constantly worried that she wouldn't be enough to make Quinn happy. That eventually he would tire of her. When she was with him, he made her feel like the most precious woman on the planet, it was because of this that caused her to worry. Why and how could she be so lucky to have such a wonderful man in her life? It was that constant question that nagged at her relentlessly, convincing her that it was only a matter of time until he got bored and moved on.

"Have you ever heard of BDSM?"

Ann swallowed a lump in her suddenly dry throat. "Yeah, I've heard of it but I don't really know much about it."

"Well, it's not really appropriate for me to explain it to you, but suffice it to say that before Sandi, I was heavily into it. I sort of gave it up for her." He laughed. "Ironic, huh? I mean I give it up for her, and it's what she really wants. Anyhow, there was a lot of yelling and screaming. I actually considered giving her one more chance. I know. It was stupid to consider, seeing as how she cheated on me at least twice. But I loved her. I didn't want to imagine my life without her. She was actually the one that ended things. She said that she didn't believe me about my lifestyle before her. She said I was just using it as a ploy to get her back. That pissed me off. I mean the Sandi that I fell in love with would have never acted so cold to me. But this new woman acted like I should and would do whatever I could to get her back. It was sort of demeaning. Bottom line is that she said I was too nice of a guy to fuck her hard like she wanted."

Ann gasped at the idea of a woman speaking to her man in such a horrible way.

"I know, so here we are. A year later and still being called 'a nice guy'. Sometimes it just plain pisses me off."

"Derek, you know that even if you gave her what she wanted that she might have still cheated on you. Because if she really loves you she wouldn't have turned to someone else, she would have talked to you and told you what she needed."

"You mean like you love Quinn?"

Ann nodded. "Yeah. I do love him. But you already know that. So, how about that drink huh?"

"Thought you weren't much of a drinker," he said as he poured two small shots.

"Well, you have the heartache of losing someone you love and I have the heartache of knowing that I'm going to lose someone that I love."

"Ann, you have to stop thinking like that. You're important to Quinn. You matter to him." He insisted.

She winced as she let the warm liquid burn down her throat. "Eew. Yeah well, I've been important to other people, too. Just never enough to keep around."

Derek hated that she was so hard on herself, so insecure of how Quinn felt about her. Soon Derek was going to have to talk to his brother. Because if Ann went on with this constant fear much longer, she was probably going to burst under the pressure.

"So, now I guess we drink." Derek raised his glass to her. "What should we drink to?"

"Hope?"

He grinned. "That sounds pretty damn good to me."

Chapter Nine

Quinn was exhausted. He pulled into his driveway and almost got out of the truck before he realized that Ann's car wasn't there. Instantly he panicked. *What could have happened to her?* He reached for his phone, already heading towards the restaurant. He listened as the phone rang and rang until finally her voicemail picked up.

"Ann where are you? Call me back."

Not wasting time Quinn dialed Derek, hoping he would know where Ann was. He glanced at the brightly lit green clock on his dashboard which read 2:45 a.m., while Derek's phone proceeded to go into his voice mail as well.

"Derek, call me man. Ann's missing."

After hanging up, Quinn glanced at his phone display. Checking to see if there was a little message symbol, hoping that he might have missed a call from her earlier that would have explained her absence. For reasons he couldn't explain, he felt a fear clawing at his gut. *What if something had happened to her?* She became so important to him that he had never stopped to think what it would be like if she was taken away.

No. Don't think like that, Quinn chided himself. *She's fine, everything's okay.* They probably just had a big rush at the restaurant and she was working late. Although knowing the time he figured that was highly unlikely. Especially seeing as how they stopped seating at nine o'clock.

Quinn turned the corner and the restaurant was finally in sight. He slowed down as he pulled into the lot. Not for safety but because he was perplexed. In the parking lot he saw Ann's and Derek's cars. Why were they still here?

He pulled his truck into a parking space and slowly got out. He could have gone to the front entrance and rang the little service bell they used for when they weren't open and the doors were locked, but he didn't. Instead he walked around to the back and found his copy of the restaurant key on his ring.

He didn't like the feeling that was overtaking him. He was scared to go inside. The ramification of what the woman he loved could be doing at close to three o'clock in the morning with his brother when she was supposed to be home sent a nauseating roil to his gut. What if he walked in on something he wasn't ready to see?

Damn it. He took a deep breath and stuck his key in the lock. Only it wasn't locked. What in the hell? He walked in the restaurant and stopped when he heard noises. Squeaking? Someone was making squeaking sounds? Then he heard Derek, breathless, gasping for breath and making incoherent sounds. *Son of a bitch!*

Quinn stormed through the restaurant until he got to the back office. He placed his arm on the door and flung it open in one giant swoosh of anger. Nothing that he imagined in his wildest fears prepared him for what he saw now.

Ann and Derek turned toward the door, startled out of their previous activity. They looked at Quinn with eyes wide, looked back at each other, and then burst back into their laughter.

Quinn looked at the two. The drunk two. They were completely skunked. The noise he had heard was them laughing so hard that they could barely breathe. So, while he was thinking the worst about the two people that meant the most to him, they were sitting in here getting shit faced.

"What in the hell is going on here?" He demanded of them.

Ann, who had her shoes off and was resting her feet comfortably on Derek's desk, turned toward him. "We're getting drunk. Wanna join us?"

Her comment must have been incredibly funny because Derek's laughter only increased as he wailed and doubled over.

"I can see that, honey. Why are you getting drunk though?"

This time it was Derek's turn. He held up his hand in a 'give me a minute' gesture. After what seemed like forever with him trying to compose himself he finally said, "Dude, your girlfriend is freaking hilarious. She has told me so many jokes tonight." Staring to laugh again, Derek did his utmost to calm himself. "Did she tell you the one about the grasshopper who walks into the bar?"

Apparently the memory of that joke was too much for Derek to handle as he burst into laughter again.

Quinn looked at Ann. "Are you two okay? How long has this been going on?"

Ann looked at her wrist, and laughed when she realized she wasn't wearing a watch.

Before Derek could pour himself another shot Quinn walked over and took the bottle from him.

"Hey, what'd you do that for?"

Quinn rolled his eyes. "Geez, I don't know, maybe because you're drunk off your ass."

Ann came up behind Quinn and wrapped her arms around him. "I missed you."

He turned and facing her he saw the desire in her eyes. "You're drunk, missy."

"True. But I'm still coherent enough to know that you're the best —"

Quinn abruptly cut her off. "Alrighty then. It looks like it's time to break up this party. Come on, yeah I know," he said as Derek groaned his disapproval. "I'm sure I should just let you finish off the bottle, but hey, I think I'll drive you home instead so you two lushes can sleep it off."

He shut off the office light as he ushered them to the back of the restaurant. He told them to wait there while he ran to the front to make sure that the entrance was locked. He got back to them in time to interrupt a debate on who was more intelligent, Elmer Fudd or Yosemite Sam.

"Okay, let's go."

After he had them stowed in the front seat he walked around to the driver's side. He had to hide his grin. Actually, Ann was kind of cute when she was drunk. He'd seen his brother drunk enough times that it made no impression, but Ann looked sexy with that warm glow of alcohol flushing her face.

He pulled out of the parking lot and almost immediately heard Derek snoring. He glanced over and sure enough Derek's head was pressed against the glass, his mouth hanging open with a tiny bit of drool escaping.

"Attractive." Quinn had said it sarcastically in reference to his brother, but Ann took it an entirely different way.

"Thanks, big boy." She got out of her seatbelt and scooted closer to him, blowing in his ear she said. "You are you know. You're so big, Quinn. I love how big you are, I love how it feels when your cock is buried deep inside of me."

"Babe. Shh. Derek's right there." But he glanced at her and saw that look in her eye that she gets sometimes. That hungry look. He should have stopped her when she brought her hand down to cup his now growing cock, but he didn't.

"Ooh, you're already getting hard. Do you know what that does to me? What you do to me?" Her voice was a seductive murmur as she started to stroke him through his jeans.

Quinn laid his head back against the head rest and gritted his teeth. He was using every amount of concentration he had to stay focused on the road ahead. "Ann, you gotta stop, honey. You're making me crazy."

She must have taken his comment as some sort of a challenge because now she was unbuttoning his jeans. "I want you, Quinn. I want this. I want to taste you." And without warning she was bent over and taking him in her mouth.

"Oh fuck, Annie." Quinn quickly pulled over to the side of the road. No way was he going to be able to concentrate on driving with her hot wet mouth sucking on him so sweetly.

"Mmm, you taste so good, Quinn."

What the hell were they doing? They couldn't do this with his brother sitting just inches away from them. "Annie, wait until we get home babe. We can't—oh shit." What was she doing? Damn, her mouth felt so good wrapped around him. She was stroking the underside with her tongue and at the same time working her fingers up and down while sucking him hard into the depths of her throat. Was it even possible to do all of that at the same time? It must have been because if sucking cock was an Olympic sport, Annie would surely bring home the gold.

Quinn heard a sound and glanced to his right. *Oh fuck.* Derek woke up and was staring at Ann give his brother head with a smile on his face. He was about to say something to stop her, but she spoke first.

"Oh, Quinn. I love this. I love taking you deep in my mouth. I love sucking on your cock until you come and spill everything that you have down my throat." She worked her tongue in a swirling motion. "It tastes so good. I love your taste. It makes me so hot, so wet."

Stop her. Fuck, Quinn, stop her, he kept telling himself. *Derek's watching for Christ's sake, but damn it, this feels so fucking good.* And her voice was driving him crazy the way she was talking to him. It was like she was fucking him with her words, too. But this was wrong. He couldn't let her go on with Derek watching. He had to stop her, "Annie, honey."

"Oh yes." She mistook his plea for lustful urgency. "Yes, Quinn! Come. I need to taste it. I need to taste you. Please."

"Babe, you've—"

"I know. God, it's so good with you. I love when you fuck me." She glanced up at him for a moment and looked into his eyes. "I swear just the thought of you being inside of me makes me so hot and wet. When you pound your big hard cock into my pussy and your balls slap against my ass I almost die from the pleasure of it."

She continued to suck and lick every inch of his hardness in between her words. She was growing impatient as she gave up her words and dove in on the sheer animalistic pleasure of fucking him with her mouth. She hadn't been kidding when she told him she needed to taste him. She did. She was wild with need for it. She could almost feel an orgasm building inside of her at the idea of him coming inside her mouth, making her swallow every last drop of him.

Shit, he was gonna come, he couldn't hold back anymore. "Annie, baby, yes. Fuck me, take me deep. Yeah, oh babe…Annie!" Quinn shouted her name as he came hard into her mouth. Spurting his seed into her throat he heard the swallowing sound she made when she allowed the very essence of him to slide down her throat and into her belly.

Quinn took a moment before glancing at his brother, who was now looking at him with a 'way to go man' look on his face. But thankfully when Annie lifted her head, Derek closed his eyes and rested his head back against the glass. Although Quinn was sure Derek would never say anything, he would need to be sure to have a little chat with his bro and make sure Annie never knew that he had witnessed that.

Annie snuggled against Quinn's chest and sighed with contentment. He wrapped his arms around her and held her close. Finally after a couple of minutes he kissed the top of her head.

"Come on honey, let's get Derek home and get ourselves home."

"Quinn?"

"Yeah, honey?" He was brushing her hair back from her face, loving how pretty she was.

"Do you know how much you…I mean, you matter to me. Do you know that?"

Her face was so serious that if it had been any other time he would have been doing cartwheels. But she was drunk, and he hated the fact that the first time she told him what he needed to hear that she would probably never even remember saying it. So instead of answering her, or telling her what he really wanted to, he kissed her and smiled at her.

No words were said as he pulled back onto the road and drove to Derek's house. Ann stayed in the truck while he helped his brother inside. After Derek had stumbled to his bed Quinn went to the kitchen got a bottle of water and some aspirin. Setting them down on Derek's night stand he told him, "You'll probably need these when you wake up."

"Thanks man."

Quinn turned to leave, but stopped. He turned back to face his brother. "That never happened. I don't want her knowing that you were awake. Understand?"

Derek nodded, "Yeah, I understand. But for the record, that was fucking amazing man."

"Shut up. Now go to sleep you freaking drunk."

Quinn locked Derek's house and got back in the truck. He looked over and saw that Ann had moved to a half sitting half laying position. Judging from her breathing she was already asleep.

He drove the rest of the way in silence, with his hand resting on her hip. Once home, he went to unlock the front door and open it. When he had that accomplished, along with turning a light on so he didn't trip and kill them both, he went back to the truck to get her.

She stirred slightly when he lifted her into his arms. "Ssh. Go back to sleep, honey," Quinn soothed her.

He carried her inside and used his foot to close the door. Walking back to the bedroom he sat her down on the bed. She had started to wake up, but the alcohol was taking over and she was swaying back and forth as he held her up, trying to take off her shirt. Once her shirt was off he moved onto her bra. When he freed her beautiful plump mounds he had to control himself from taking one of her rosy nipples into his mouth until the center formed into erect little points. Because damn if they didn't look appetizing.

Next he gently laid her down and undid the button to her jeans and slid down her zipper. He yanked them down her legs and pulled them off at the ankles. Next came her socks. All that was left were her panties. A red little satin and lace number that given her current condition he would have left on her and tucked her under the covers. He would have, if he hadn't seen the darkened part of the satin where her wetness had seeped out of her. She told him while she was giving him the most incredible blow job that she would get wet just thinking about him. Obviously, she hadn't been lying because his hand reached over and cupped the wet heat. He hesitated, waited for a small smile of encouragement from her before he massaged her through her panties.

"Oh, Jesus." She was soaking wet. He couldn't help himself. He tore her panties down her legs in one fluid movement. He heard her moan and arch her hips up as he brought his mouth down and slid his tongue inside her already saturated folds. Damn, she tasted good. He loved the taste of her anytime, but knowing that all of this sweetness was just from the sheer act of her enveloping his cock with her velvety soft mouth was so fucking erotic.

Ann whimpered and whispered his name. "Quinn, yes. Oh…mmm…"

Annie's legs wrapped around his neck and he had to smile at her ardor. Sometimes she was so shy and uncertain of her sexuality and other times she was this brazen woman who took charge and didn't stop until she got what she wanted. It was an incredibly sexy contradiction.

"My clit, Quinn. Please. I need you to suck on my clit. I need to come…oh."

He did as she asked and took her clit in his mouth, tonguing it and teasing it until finally suckling on it like a starving man. Her hips shot up from the bed and ground against him as she screamed his name.

Explosions tore through her body. A white hot flame of burning liquid shot through her soul and poured out of her as she felt Quinn lapping up her release. She was in a slight haze from the alcohol, but that had nothing to do with the feeling that overcame her. She wanted to cry from the joy that he gave her. He made everything so right, so complete. He was absolutely everything to her. She only wished and prayed that she would be able to keep him. Because the thought of being without Quinn was a pain that she just didn't want to consider.

Chapter Ten

"Ohhh. Quinn please, turn off that light. It's too bright!" Ann groaned her request as she pulled the pillow up over her head.

Quinn was in the bathroom and peeked his head out at her. "That's the sunlight, babe. Can't turn it off, sorry."

She pulled the pillow off of her head just slightly and looked at him. She had to squint at the small amount of light that was seeping through the blinds. "Why is it so bright? Are we plummeting to the Sun on a cataclysmic course of destruction or something?"

He wiped the remainder of shaving cream off of his face and walked into the bedroom. He crawled on the bed next to her and wrapped his arms around her, planting a small kiss to the tip of her nose.

"No, we're not on a collision course with the sun, but I imagine that's what your head feels like right about now. Here, take these." He leaned over the bed to the night stand and grabbed the water bottle and aspirin that he set there earlier.

She swallowed them and winced at the energy it took for such a small task. "Thanks."

"Sure. You okay?"

She nodded yes, and then quickly shook her head no. "I don't know. I feel pretty bad."

He laughed at her. "I can imagine. You two were pretty far gone last night. What happened anyway?"

She looked at him as she tried to think of an answer. What *had* happened? She knew she had been at the restaurant. There was some laughing, no wait, no, that part came later. They were in the kitchen at first and then Derek got upset. Then she…oh, that's right. She turned her head back to Quinn from its protective position under her hands.

"Derek was upset. He told me about Sandi."

Quinn hadn't expected that to be the reason for their dive into oblivion. "Oh shit. Are you serious? I thought he was getting over that."

Ann shrugged. "I think he tries and usually does a pretty good job, but last night some people were razzing him about what a nice guy he is, and—"

"Oh great. I can imagine how well that went over. That's like the freaking thorn in his side."

"I found that out. Anyway, when it was time to leave, he had already started drinking. We talked for a while, he told me everything. And for the record, I'm not a big fan of this Sandi girl."

"Me either hon. So, how'd you guys end up getting shit faced?"

She expelled a breath and held her hands to the sides of her head, massaging her temples. Quinn saw her discomfort and moved her hands away as he proceeded to massage her aching head for her.

"Mmm…that feels good. Well, at first we were just going to have a toast to hope, you know, kind of like a 'there's other fish in the sea' sort of thing. But one drink turned into two, then two turned into three and I think I lost count after like number seven or eight, or maybe it was nine. I'm not sure. All I know is that I never want to see one of those black and white bottles ever again."

Quinn leaned over and kissed her forehead. In a whiny voice he said, "Poor baby."

"Don't tease. It's not funny."

"Okay, I'm sorry. Listen, do you think you can eat anything? I can make you something."

She cringed at the thought of food. "I don't think so Quinn." She took his hand. "But thank you."

"Sure thing, honey. You get some rest. I think I'm gonna go check on Derek. He doesn't do so well with hangovers. He's probably yakked all over his house by now."

"Thanks for the visual."

He patted her head and got off the bed. "Go to sleep, I'll be back in an hour or so."

"Quinn?"

He turned back from the closet, while he finished dressing, pulling his t-shirt over his head. "Yeah. You need me to get you something?"

She shook her head. "No, I was just wondering did I…I mean I thought I remembered…no never mind. It's stupid."

"No it's not, tell me. Did you what?"

She bunched her brows together as she hesitated, wondering if she really wanted the truth. "Did I give you a blow job while your brother was sitting right next to us?"

He chuckled, "Yep. You sure did, honey. And I got to tell you, pretty damn awesome."

"Oh, God. I have to quit now. How can I ever look at him again?"

Quinn did a little internal conscious check. He reminded himself the little white lie he was about to tell was for her own good. "No he was passed out babe. He had no idea."

"Are you sure?"

Just a little white lie, no big deal. "Totally. Now go to sleep okay?"

She grinned at him before lying back down. "Bye."

She rolled over and faced away from him. A small part of him hoped that maybe she remembered her serious moment last night, when she looked at him and tried to tell him how important he was to her. He needed to know her true feelings when alcohol wasn't involved. He needed to know that she felt that way regardless of how many drinks she had. But apparently that was just wishful thinking on his part.

Twenty minutes later, Quinn walked into his brother's house and had to cover his face with his shirt to mask the stench. He headed down the hallway to his brothers bedroom and then into his bathroom. When there he was in all of his glory, praying to the porcelain god.

"Oh Jesus, man. Look at this place. You couldn't have at least made it to the toilet."

Derek just looked up at his brother in disgust. "Fuck off."

Quinn reached his hand into the shower and turned it on. "Now, now. Is that any way to treat your brother? Especially the brother who drove your drunk ass safely home last night?"

"Careful, I still have some ammunition. Would you like me to tell your *Annie* that you allowed her to suck you off while I watched?" He exaggerated her name when he said it because he had no idea that Quinn called her that until last night. It was a neat little tid bit of information to give his brother shit about.

"You breathe a word to her and I will personally see to it that you no longer have any balls. Besides, you better be nice to me, because while you're in that shower washing that unbelievably horrific stench off of your sorry ass, I will be cleaning this shit up."

Derek actually softened for a moment. "You know for a little shit brother, you're not so bad."

"That's what I've been freaking telling you my whole life. Now come on, get in there." Quinn helped Derek to his feet and cringed. "Shit man, how'd you get puke on the back of your head?"

Derek just grinned, "I'm a creative son of a bitch, that's how."

"Whatever, just get in the damn shower."

Quinn walked in the bedroom and sat on the edge of the bed. He pulled his phone from his pocket and dialed Ann.

"Hello?" She moaned into the phone.

Quinn winced. Apparently she already fell back asleep. "Sorry, babe, I didn't mean to wake you. Listen, I'm gonna be a little longer than I thought. Derek puked *everywhere*, and I mean everywhere. It looks like a Goddamn crime scene over here. He's in the shower now.

I've got to help him clean it up otherwise he'll never be able to have another woman over again. This stench is starting to seep into the walls."

"Oh geez. Do you need some help?"

"No, that's not why I'm calling. I just wanted to let you know I'd be a while and I just wanted to make sure you'd call me if you needed anything." *And I love you*, he silently added. "Your car is at the restaurant so you're kind of stranded for now until I get back there."

She smiled through the phone at his thoughtfulness. "Thanks, Quinn. I'll be fine. Just take care of Derek, okay?"

"All right. Sorry I woke you."

"Bye." They said in unison, before both hanging up.

Quinn returned his phone to his pocket and placed his hands down to push himself off of the bed. What the…? He looked down and saw that he had missed a little present his brother had left for him. But he found it now. His once clean hand was now spread in and bathing in his brother's vomit.

* * * *

Two hours later, Ann got out of the shower and dressed. She felt a little better, but definitely not her best, so a simple comb through of her hair and some cotton shorts along with a shirt was the extent of her grooming. She walked toward the kitchen with the intent to try and make a go of some sort of food.

She perused the contents of the pantry, refrigerator and then the freezer. She couldn't find anything that looked good. What she really wanted were some waffles, but the last of the frozen ones were eaten two days ago. And it's not like she could make any from scratch—or could she? She remembered seeing some pancake batter in the pantry. She went back and rummaged through the contents until she found the package. And as if God had answered her prayers right there on the back were the instructions for modifying the ingredients to make waffle batter instead of pancake batter.

A smiled curved her lips up when she remembered Quinn telling her that he had some kitchen gadgets that he hardly ever used in the spare bedroom closet. She marched down the hall on a mission. *Please let there be a waffle maker,* she thought to herself. She opened the closet door, dug around some of the boxes inside and voila. There it was a small little waffle maker.

Once she had put everything back in its place in the closet, she shut it and turned to head back toward the kitchen. She stopped in the hallway when she heard a crash. Walking back into the spare room she opened the closet again to see what had fallen. She was surprised when she saw what it was.

Her mouth hung open in shock as she stared at the contents. Spilled out on the floor in front of her was an assortment of magazines and videos which left little to the imagination. But those weren't what had completely captivated her. Lying next to a video called *Anal Entry* was a string of beads, but they weren't the kind you'd expect your aunt to wear to a barbeque. No these definitely were not beads to a necklace.

Ann bent over and picked them up. The length of the string was probably about a foot long with jelly like beads spaced evenly about every inch or so and on the end there was a little ring, like one you would see on a yo-yo. She was completely perplexed as she stared at the strange string. She looked down and saw something sticking out from underneath one of the magazines. She set the string of beads down and picked up the magazine. She gasped when she saw it.

She knew what it was. She'd heard of them before, even seen pictures of them. But never had she actually seen one. As if her curiosity had taken over for her she was now bending down to take the phallic-shaped item in her hand. Ann held it up and studied it, intrigued by the jelly like look of it. It was purple and smaller than

Quinn. Actually it was smaller than most men, if not all. It was then that she realized that it wasn't an ordinary sex toy. It had one purpose.

She looked down at all of the items and found herself dropping to her knees to study everything. She set the purple dildo down and picked up a magazine titled *Sex Toys for Him & Her*. Ann tried to ignore the rush of heat that slammed through her body and shot to her core at the sight of what was on the inside cover.

It was a couple in bed. Which would have been fine, except the woman was tied to the headboard, on her knees while the man in the picture was behind her fucking her. While you couldn't be sure exactly where the man was taking her the advertisement on the top of the page left little to the imagination. It read quite simply, *Take your Anal Sex to New Heights of Pleasure with Liquid Silver Lubrication.*

Anal Sex? Was this what Quinn was into? He had never tried anything with her. Nor had he ever even talked about it. Sure he had surprised her by rubbing his fingers down there a couple of times, but that was as far as it had gone. And he knew that she wasn't into that so it wasn't like—*oh no.* It suddenly hit her.

Quinn *was* into this. He liked this, wanted this, and maybe even needed this. And she had made it more than clear that she would never consider it. So he had stashed his 'collection' away so she wouldn't see it. How could she have been so stupid? She knew something like this was going to happen. Her biggest fear was that Quinn would have needs that she wouldn't be able to fulfill. And now she was even more convinced than ever that he would get bored with her and move on.

She didn't want that to happen. She wanted Quinn and she wanted to make him happy. But how could she do that when she would never, could never give him what he so obviously needed? She thought for a moment about Derek and what happened with him and Sandi. Would they still be together if they trusted each other enough to open up about their deepest, darkest fantasies?

Ann didn't want to lose Quinn because she was unwilling to consider everything that mattered to him. She stared at the advertisement for a minute before picking up the video that had earlier caught her eye. She touched it, debating upon whether or not to actually pick it up and watch it. Finally, she picked it up and ran in the living room. If she gave it too much thought she would chicken out. So she put the tape in the VCR and hit play.

Ann sat on the couch directly across from the television and waited as the opening credits ran. Finally it began, and it didn't take long, merely a couple of lines of dialogue and the couple on the screen was already heavy into the foreplay. So far she hadn't seen anything that had repulsed her or made her feel uncomfortable. She relaxed a little as she continued to stare at the television.

She licked her lips unconsciously when the woman took the large cock in her mouth and sucked on it like she would die if she didn't get all of him inside her mouth. Is that what she looked like when she did it to Quinn? She was surprised by her own internal response; she sure as hell hoped so because while the woman was doing it she looked damn sexy.

The couple moved and was now on a couch. The lady moved into an odd position leaning over the edge of the couch. Her arms were outstretched along the backside and Ann watched in anticipation as the man came up behind the woman and rubbed himself against her bare ass.

Ann was shocked when she heard herself moan. The man had leaned over and grabbed a small tube from the table. He flipped the cap open and squirted a liberal amount of a jelly-like substance on the woman's ass, causing her to rock her hips and move herself against his erection.

Was it getting hotter in here? Ann squirmed a little in her position on the couch as she watched the man rub the shiny lubrication all around her rear and finally dip it into the tiny puckered opening. Jesus. He's going to take her there. How could she? He's too big to take in such a small hole. And what was wrong with her? Her pulse was pounding and she could feel her womb clenching in arousal.

Was she actually getting turned on by the idea of anal sex? *No,* she answered her own question. The idea of it had always scared her and, well, that was it. She was going to say that it had repulsed her, but really that wasn't true. Just the idea of the discomfort and pain were the only things that truly bothered her about it. But the lady on the television was writing beneath the man's ministrations as he worked first one, then two and then three fingers in and out of her tiny hole. There was no mistaking it. Ann was getting more than turned on by the idea of it. She was already wet. Unbeknownst to her she had started to drag her hand down to her shorts to test just how wet she truly was when she heard a key hit the door.

Never, ever in her entire life did Ann ever remember moving that quickly. Because she jumped off the couch and was running toward the VCR when the door opened. Quinn stopped dead in his tracks and stared at the scene before him.

Chapter Eleven

Neither one of them said anything for several moments. They just stared at each other. Quinn was the first one to break the silence. He closed the door and put his hands on his hips. "Ann. Did you…where did you get that?"

Was he talking? Because all she felt right now was complete mortification at being caught watching a porno in her boyfriends living room all by herself. *God, what he must think of her?* And the box. *Oh great,* the box was still sitting in the back bedroom on the floor. *Crap, how was she going to get out of this one?* She didn't get a chance to answer her own question because they were both startled by the sound of the women screaming on the television, begging to be fucked harder.

Quinn walked over to the VCR and hit stop, then eject. He slowly set the tape down on the end table and turned towards her.

"Ann, I—"

"Quinn, I—"

They both spoke at the same time, subsequently silencing each other at the same time as well. So there they stood again in awkward silence.

Quinn expelled a very large breath. "Ann, I never meant for you to see these things."

That was actually what she worried about. He wasn't going to be honest with her and tell her what he really and truly wanted. "I didn't mean to. I wasn't snooping."

He shook his head. "I didn't think you were, hon. And I wouldn't care if you did. I have nothing to hide. Well, I mean not anymore."

Damn it. Why hadn't he gotten rid of this crap? Actually, he had forgotten about it. It had been awhile since he had a woman that was daring enough to take both his size and his appetite.

"I wanted waffles."

He cocked his head to one side in confusion. "Waffles?"

"Well yeah, they sounded good, and the waffle maker was in the back bedroom closet. I guess I didn't put something away right because, um, a box fell and…well I would have just put it back, but it sort of fell on its side and stuff spilled out."

Fucking great! "Ann, honey." He went to her. He didn't want her to think he was some sort of kinky pervert that was going to try to force her to do these things. He knew how she felt about them. And he was okay with that. He loved her. If giving up a fantasy or two to be with her was the price he would have to pay, then he figured that was a small sacrifice.

"I'm sorry, Quinn. I didn't mean to invade your personal life."

He framed her face in his hands and stopped her from turning away from him. "Honey, you are my personal life."

She bit down on her bottom lip nervously. She had so many questions. Never before had she been curious about anal sex before, but now as she felt her wetness at the apex of her thighs she knew that for whatever reason her body was very intrigued.

"Honey, I'm sorry." He told her, hating that she had found his secret out.

"Sorry? Why?"

"I didn't want you to worry." He hesitated a second before he continued. "I don't need things like that. I don't want those things."

He didn't? Then why did he have all this stuff? "Quinn, maybe we should…"

"No, listen to me Ann. This stuff," He moved away from her and picked up the tape, "is from my past. It has nothing to do with you and I, okay?"

She listened to his heartfelt speech. He cared about her, that much she was sure of. But did he not care about her enough to share his deepest fantasies with her. She had told him some of hers. Heck that was how they even got together in the first place. But was that the real difference? She was in love with him, so she knew that he was the only one she could ever share her fantasies with. But maybe that's what was missing for him, he wasn't in love with her, so therefore he couldn't tell his fantasies to her. Because after all was said and done she just wasn't *the one*.

"Quinn, follow me." She walked out of the living room and back to the bedroom. She waited for him to join her before she said anymore. When he was standing in the doorway she continued, "How can you expect me to believe that this doesn't matter."

Damn it. He would not lose her to his sexual appetites. He would give up anything to be with her, except for making love to her. That was a deal breaker. Because he needed her just as much as he needed air, water and food.

"It *doesn't* matter. Look maybe we should sit down and talk about things."

Ann didn't like the seriousness of his tone. She had found the proof of his darkest desires, and now he wanted to talk. Was he going to end things with her? "I don't want to talk about things. I just want you to tell me the truth about what you want."

"I want you." He flung the video, which was still in his hand and threw it on top of the pile on the floor. Quinn pulled her close to his body and kissed her. He put everything he had into it. He didn't want there to be any room left for doubt. He fisted his hand in the back of her hair and used his other to cup her breast. She wasn't wearing a bra and he could feel her nipple harden with his slightest touch.

Ann whimpered with instant need for him. She was already confused, worried and aroused all at the same time from what she had seen on that video, but his touch was sending her over the edge. She wanted him. Now. But more than that, she wanted him in her future. She pulled away from him.

"Quinn, no. Stop." She insisted.

"What? No…baby, listen to me okay?" He took her hand and molded it against his erection. "Can't you see how much I need you? That's what only you can do to me. Not those other things. Just you, babe." He kissed her again, using every trick he had learned during their time together on how to turn her into a puddle of aching need.

"Quinn, it's important to me, I need you to tell me. Why do you have those things?" He was doing that thing with his tongue again. He slid it along her neck and across to her shoulder, burning her skin with his skillful attention, while he drove her wild with passion.

"Those things don't matter, honey. Please, let me have you." He wasn't really asking for permission, because he was already pulling down her shorts. When he slid his hand into her panties he actually gasped in shock. He looked at her with shock on his face. "Annie?" He looked at her.

She licked her lips nervously. She knew what had shocked him. She was always wet and ready for Quinn, but that video had literally almost made her come. She was completely drenched. "Quinn, I…"

"God, baby. Do you know how wet you are?" His desire was written all over his face, as he plunged two fingers inside of her. His eyes leered at her as he watched the pleasure wash over her face at the invasion.

"Quinn…mmm…yes…" Somehow, she wasn't sure how, but she remembered what her main priority was. She pulled away from him and stepped back. "No!" She was breathless, but she remained firm, "Quinn, I *need* you to tell me why you have those things."

What was going on with her? She had never pushed him away before just so they could talk. Her little discovery was freaking her out more than he realized. He had to prove to her that she mattered more to him than any kink ever could. He ignored her protests as he walked towards her. He grabbed onto her and flung her around.

Ann was startled by his roughness and more than a little excited by it. She felt him grind his hardness against her bottom. It suddenly felt so good. The intimate contact of the two body parts rubbing up against one another. *Why won't he talk to me about it?* She worried herself with the question as she heard Quinn's zipper slide. She instinctively arched her body into his when she felt him push her forward, forcing her to break a potential fall by dropping her hands to the small dresser. Her panties were being dragged down her legs while she spread her legs to accept him. He had only taken her from behind once before and it had felt good. But she had been nervous. Not now though, now she wanted and needed the feel of him taking her from behind.

As if he was listening to her thoughts, Quinn slammed into her. He had never taken her so quickly before. He instantly hit the deepest parts of her pussy. Her once throbbing womb was now a river of pure desire and lust for no one and nothing but him. How did he always manage to make it better than the last time? She was moaning and writhing with him, rocking her body against his. She was lost in the sound of flesh slapping against flesh. She could feel his balls as they hit against her clit with every hard thrust. He had been inside her for all of a minute and she was already so close to her orgasm.

* * * *

Quinn looked down at her body as he slammed in and out of her. Her rounded ass was driving him crazy. He grasped onto her hips to keep himself from taking a finger and dipping it inside the sweet abyss of her forbidden hole. *God, he wanted to fuck her there.* To make her come while he was buried deep inside her in the most taboo of ways. But he couldn't. His Ann was perfect for him in many ways, but she wasn't into that. And having her without all of his little fetishes was more important than not having her at all.

"Quinn!" Ann came in a rush of pure ecstasy.

He slammed into her once more as he felt her liquid heat pour all over his cock. He grabbed onto her tighter as he lost himself inside of her. Convulsing his body and jerking his hips as he spurt into her.

"Oh damn, babe. You are amazing." He was massaging his hands up and down her back, still inside of her when he remembered the items scattered on the floor. He had to put an end to her worries now. He didn't want her to ever wonder what he needed or wanted again.

Quinn slid out of her and turned her around. "Does that answer your question about what I need or want?"

* * * *

She nodded. She was still coming down from her orgasm, but she knew he was lying to her. He wanted those things, apparently she did too, but he didn't want to share that part of himself with her. And that hurt more than she could ever explain. She was about to say something when he walked from the room, pulling up his pants.

She stood there, half dressed and waited. She could hear him coming back down the hall towards the bedroom. He walked in with a trash bag and headed for the pile.

"Quinn, what are you doing?"

He looked up at her from his position on the floor. "I told you, this stuff doesn't matter. It's my past. I should have thrown it away a long time ago. So that's what I'm going to do now."

Was he that desperate to keep a part of himself closed off from her that he would throw away something that was obviously so very important to him? "Quinn, why? Why can't you just tell me what you really—"

"Ann!" He snapped at her. He didn't mean to. He was just so agitated. He wasn't going to lose her to some stupid kink that he couldn't get past. It was his problem, not hers. "I'm sorry, honey. I just don't want you to think about this stuff. It has nothing to do with us. I'm sorry you ever saw it."

And there it was. All the proof that she needed. He not only wasn't going to tell her what he wanted or needed, but he was sorry that she had found out anything about it. She was the last person he wanted to share that with. For a moment, she let her mind wander to a bad place, where Quinn was getting what he needed with someone else. But she quickly dismissed that notion. He might not be willing to share who he was with her, but she knew that as long as she had him he would remain monogamous.

She watched him as he continued to throw the items in the trash and wondered how long she would have him for.

Quinn tied the bag and took it to the garage. When he came back in he still saw the uncertainty in her eyes that she had ever since he came home and found that she had discovered his stash. He wanted to take that look away, make her happy. He went to her to hold her when she pulled away.

Sure, she put a smile on her face when she said, "I'll go make the waffles now," but he could sense her withdrawal. He'd seen it before, too. Things would be fine between them and then something would happen and she would become sad and distant. He wished he knew what was causing her to pull away from him. He wished for so many things. He wanted nothing more than to hold her and tell her just how important she was to him.

To hell with his kinky fetishes and everything else. All he wanted, all he needed was Ann. *His Annie.*

Chapter Twelve

Quinn and Ann were finishing their waffles when the phone rang. "No, I've got it. You relax." He got up and headed across the room.

"Hello." Quinn cringed. "Shit you sound terrible man. Didn't that nap help at all?"

"Uhhh…seeing as how there was no nap and a group of a million percussionists were banging in my head, I'm not feeling so hot." Derek groaned the words through the phone.

Quinn laughed at his brother. But Ann had been watching him and gave him the 'be nice' look so he composed himself. "So what do you need? Did you throw up in the back of your hair again? Need someone to wash it out?"

Derek snickered. "You think you're pretty damn funny, don't you asshole?"

"As a matter of fact, I do."

If looks could kill and someone had invented a way to transmit those glares via the telephone wire, then Quinn would be one very dead brother. "Well, I don't. Listen, I can't go into the restaurant tonight."

"What? Shit, Derek. I've got to be at the Roadhouse. You know how busy we are on Saturdays."

"I know and stop yelling damn it. I can't help it. Every time I move, I feel the need to throw up. And besides, I wasn't asking for you to take care of the restaurant. I was wondering how Ann was feeling. Do you think she's up to it?"

Quinn looked over at Ann. She had gotten up and cleared the table. She was now bent over and loading the dishwasher. Damn, she had a fine ass. What he wouldn't give to be able to tell her what he really wanted to do to her. And he was pretty sure he would give his right arm if she told him that she wanted it, too. Just the idea of spreading the seam of her ass and sinking into the sweet oblivion of her forbidden hole was his deepest fantasy.

"Quinn? You listening to me or what? Can Ann handle it?"

Can Ann handle it? How did Derek know what he had been thinking about? *Oh wait, no, he means the restaurant.*

"Hang on." Quinn set the phone down and came up behind her. "Hey, hon. Derek wants to know if you feel up to taking care of the restaurant tonight." Quinn yelled louder. "Because he's a candy ass who can't handle his liquor."

"Go to Hell!" Derek yelled through the phone.

Ann rolled her eyes at the brothers loving attitude towards one another. But she smiled anyway. "Yeah. I can handle it. Except I've never been there when he first opens up. I don't know the security code either. Could you come with me and show me what needs to be done?"

"Sure, babe. You should be sainted, you know that right?" Quinn placed a small kiss to her nose and walked back over to the phone.

"Yeah, she says she'll do it. She's saving your sorry ass is what she's doing. But whatever, not everyman can be as great as me." Quinn pointed out rather smugly.

"Whatever. Keep thinking that man. Because when I'm well I'm gonna kick your ass."

"As if? You could try, but I promise you would not be successful."

Derek groaned a little more in frustration and pain. "Fine. Geez, I don't have the mental energy to spar with you right now. Just show her what to do, okay? I'm gonna go throw up right now."

"Wait. Remember you wanna hit that white circular thing in the bathroom. The one with the little silver handle." Quinn laughed. He loved to mock his brother.

"You probably can't see it, but there's a very big birdie aimed in your direction. I'm hanging up now."

Quinn hung up the phone and turned to find Ann smiling at him. "What?"

She shook her head laughing. "Nothing. You two. You love each other like crazy but you give one another nothing but crap constantly."

"First of all, let me just state for the record, I don't love him *like crazy*." He gave her a lazy half smile. "We're brothers. It's what we do. Didn't you and your sister ever fight?"

She looked at him, surprised that he'd asked. They never really talked about her family. She knew that was because she usually changed the subject. The truth was she didn't really like talking about her family. So, changing the subject always seemed like the logical thing to do.

They had talked in great deal about his family. He told her about the horrible time when they found out that his Aunt Connie, Derek's mother, had an inoperable brain cancer. And how sad it was for them all to watch her suffer through the pain of her final weeks because the morphine the doctors gave her barely put a dent in the agony that she was suffering.

He told her how hard it was for him to watch his parents grieve for her, knowing that they were doing so in very different ways and for extremely different reasons. And Derek. Poor Derek had apparently had a pretty hard time of it. By Ann's estimations, it would seem that he probably had met his ex-girlfriend, Sandi within a year of his mother's passing.

"Ann? Where'd you go, hon?" He brushed the back of his hand down her cheek.

"Would you believe me if I said a land far, far away?" She smirked.

"Probably not." But he grinned anyway. "What's up? Does it bother you that I brought up your sister? I know we never talk about your family, I just thought that since we're living together and we're getting… I just didn't think it'd be that big of a deal." *Damn. Why won't she open up to me?* Quinn wondered.

"No Quinn, it's not that. It's not really a big deal. It's just that I don't have the fondest childhood memories and even though my sister and I grew up together it was always pretty much survival of the fittest you know?"

Actually no, he said silently. *Because you never tell me anything.* "Why don't you tell me what you mean? Was it that bad?"

She had briefly told him one night when they were lying in bed that her father had been an alcoholic and her mother was never around much because she was always screwing around on her dad. She mentioned a sister that was a couple years older than her, but that was it. That was the extent of what he knew about her family life.

She shook her head at his question. "No. I mean it's not like there was abuse or anything like that. It just sort of sucked. I can't ever remember really having parents. I mean, I did. They were physically there, but emotionally they were pretty much nonexistent. Aside from trying to control my life, I hardly ever talked to my dad." She shrugged. "Geez, I sound depressing huh."

She walked away from Quinn, and he knew that she was attempting to change the subject. But he didn't want her to. He wanted to know everything about her; everything that happened to her that brought her to who and what she was today.

"Ann?" He waited for her to turn back and face him. Once she did he noticed a barely visible shimmer in her eye. "What is it, honey? Talk to me."

Ann looked up to the ceiling and maybe even the God's above for the strength to deal with his concerned questions. It wasn't that she didn't trust him enough to share her memories. They just kind of sucked. And she didn't always like talking about them. It was just easier to forget.

Then of course there was the fact that every time he treated her so important, like he cared so much, she would just fall deeper in love with him. She tried not to laugh at herself when she sometimes wished he would be a jerk. An insensitive jerk that would be so easy to not love. But that was even more ludicrous. Because she couldn't ever imagine herself not loving Quinn Travis.

"Annie, please. Trust me." He delicately brushed his hands up and down her arms in a soothing fashion.

"Oh, Quinn. It's not that I don't trust you. I do. I just didn't have the happy family upbringing that you did."

Her statement made Quinn laugh. "Happy? Well, I don't know about that. My Mom and Aunt Connie sure cried a lot. My Dad put a damper on the whole happy family image."

"Yeah I know. But you guys all loved each other. I mean despite everything you knew that you were loved."

Quinn was shocked by her comment. He knew that she didn't have the happiest memories but he never realized it was so bad that she hadn't felt loved.

"I'm so sorry, honey. I never knew that you felt that way." He wrapped his arms around her and placed a kiss on top of her head.

"It's okay. How could you know?"

He looked down at her. "You're right. I couldn't have known, because you won't tell me."

Ann stared up into his eyes. "Quinn, I—"

He quickly cut her off. "Tell me, Annie. Talk to me and tell me about your life." He smirked. "We'll call it the pre-Quinn era."

Ann looked up at him and had to smile. He was so handsome and when he laid on the charm, there was no denying him anything he wanted.

"Okay. What would you like to know?"

Quinn was surprised by her sudden change of heart. He figured he'd have to really hound her for a while before she bent. "Come on, we'll go sit in the living room." He led her to the couch, turned his body to face hers and laced their fingers together.

"Tell me, honey. Start wherever you want. I just want to hear about your life." *Because I love you so much that I need to feel connected to you, close to you.*

Ann shrugged, "I don't know where to begin. I mean, no actually I do know. I can tell you what changed it. What made everything go from good to really bad."

Quinn quirked a brow up at what she said. For whatever reason he just assumed it was always bad. He wondered what could have happened to their family to cause such a change.

"See, it wasn't always just me and my sister. We had a brother. He was three years older than me. One year older than Susan. That's my sister." She removed her hand from Quinn's so that she could run her fingers through her hair. "See, when I was five, and my brother, Connor, was eight, he was riding his bike home from a friend's house. It was just a block away. Really it was more like around the corner."

Ann shook her head at the memory. "You could see his friend's driveway from our side window. So, it wasn't like it was really that far or anything. Sorry, I'm telling you this like you're accusing us of something. It's just that when it happened a lot of people gave my parents a hard time. People told them that their lax attitude toward their children's safety had been the real cause of it. Not that drunk driver."

Oh God. "Annie, honey, I'm so sorry. Your brother was killed by a drunk driver?"

She nodded. "Yeah. It was sad, because that day my brother wasn't the only one that died. My parents did, too." She looked at Quinn. "They were really great at one time. But when Connor died, a piece of them went too. Actually not just a piece, more like their soul. They just sort of fell apart. They didn't know how to help each other."

Ann took a big breath before she continued, "After a while they just stopped trying. Dad had already long since taken to the bottle for comfort and mom was so lonely that I think she slept with other men to feel some sort of affection. Dad never talked to her. He ignored us all really, except when he was telling us what we could or couldn't do. I think it just got too much for mom. That's why I think she killed herself. I mean—"

"Woah. What did you say, honey?"

She saw the stunned look on his face. She hadn't even realized until that very moment that he'd had no idea that her mother was dead. "Sorry. I guess I forgot to mention that. Three weeks after my sixteenth birthday I came home and found mom lying in a pile of her own vomit. She was already dead. Had been for hours. She took about thirty of those over the counter sleeping pills." A tear escaped from her eye as she remembered what she had walked in on that day.

Quinn reached for her and pulled her onto his lap. Holding her tight, he said, "Oh babe, I'm so sorry that you had to go through that." And he was. The idea that Ann felt any pain at all tore at his heart.

She sniffled a little as she held her tears below the surface. "It's okay. I mean I was kind of numb to everything by then. But do you want to know the really sad part though?"

There's more? "Sure, honey. Tell me."

"I wasn't surprised. I just got home from school. I walked in the house and I remember getting the strange feeling that something was off, but I ignored it. I was heading back to my bedroom when I saw her lying there in her bed. It still seems so clear to me, like it was yesterday. I can still remember my first reaction to when I saw her lying there. I thought, so today was the day. She finally decided to go through with it."

Quinn closed his eyes on the cold and bitter sound of her voice. "She told you she was going to do it?"

"No, it's just that I knew, you know. She was dead long before she ever actually took her own life."

Quinn held her closer. "I can't imagine what that must have been like for you, babe. What about your dad and your sister? How did they take the news?" He realized that it was a stupid question. Because how else would you handle a family member committing suicide?

Buried in the crook of his arm she muffled her reply. "Susan was like me. She sort of saw it coming." She looked up at him. "But my dad. God, Quinn. I thought the worst pain I'd ever see him in was the day that Connor died. But it all came rushing back to me that day. The horrific sounds that tore from his throat."

Ann sat up and ran her hands through her hair. "God. I haven't thought about this in such a long time."

Quinn rubbed a hand up and down her back. "I'm sorry, honey. I know I keep saying that, but I don't know what else I can say."

"It's okay, Quinn. There's nothing you can say. There's nothing anyone can do or say. It just is." She shook her head. "Sometimes I don't know what was worse. When Connor died, when my mom killed herself, or when my dad realized much too late that he still loved his wife and his family."

Quinn nodded, knowing that no words could possibly change how she was feeling at that moment. They were silent for a few minutes as Quinn continued to rub her back. He wanted to do something, anything for her. But he felt completely helpless.

"Annie?"

She turned to him. "Yes."

"What happened to your dad? Do you see him, or talk to him ever?"

"I used to. After my Mom died we all started talking again. Dad slowed down on the drinking, but he never stopped completely. Time went by and neither my sister nor I realized it, but before either one of us knew what was going on he was drinking heavily again. It was hard. I think that he tried in his own way. I really do. Susan doesn't though. She blames him."

"Why? How could he be responsible for what happened to your brother?" Quinn wondered.

"No, not with Connor. But everything else. See, she thinks that if Dad was stronger and he was there for Mom, then maybe they could have been there for each other."

"What do you think?"

Ann expelled a huge breath at his question. A question that she'd asked herself many times before. It was also a question she didn't want to answer because despite everything, he was still her dad and the only parent she had left.

"I think that it doesn't matter what I think. That what happened can't be changed and being angry at my dad, my mom or even the drunk driver that killed Connor won't change what happened. It sucks. But that's just the way that it is."

Quinn was both surprised and in awe at her attitude toward such a clearly horrible event. Anyone else would surely be traumatized, but not Ann. She was stronger than that. God, he loved her.

* * * *

Things were getting too serious. She was showing a side to herself that he probably wasn't going to want to deal with. He would think she was needy and emotional. She was tired of the tension hovering around the room at the somber topic. She didn't want to think about it anymore. She just wanted to forget that part of her life because sometimes it was just too painful to rehash. "So, I guess we better go get ready so we can open the restaurant."

"Yeah, I supposed you're right. Come on, the last one in the shower is a rotten egg." He got up off of the couch and pulled her up.

Ann laughed, "Rotten egg huh? That's really original, Quinn. Did you think that one up all by yourself?"

"Shush woman, come on let's go." So they headed towards the shower to get ready to leave. As usual, one thing had led to another, then that thing led to another and an hour later Quinn was telling her, "we better get going and soon. If we don't hurry we're going to be late."

"It's not my fault that you have an overactive sex drive," she teased him.

"Actually it is one hundred percent completely your fault." He wrapped his arms around her. "Yep, totally your fault, you're too damn sexy for me to resist." Only Quinn wasn't teasing. He was dead serious.

An hour later they arrived at the restaurant. Quinn gave her his key and showed her how to unlock and lock the door since it was always a little tricky. He went over the alarm system with her in great detail and also explained about the panic button, should, God forbid they were to ever have a robbery or something like that.

It was fifteen minutes before the first of the staff were due to arrive when Quinn waggled his brows at her suggestively, "You know honey. I've always harbored a secret fantasy about this place."

Ann was sincerely shocked. "My God, Quinn. Where does it all come from? I mean women can come over and over again with no problem. But don't men need some sort of rejuvenation period or something?" She laughed in spite of herself.

Quinn walked towards her, "You see honey, most men probably do. But I'm, how could I explain it? Extra special. See I have sort of like a super hero cock."

Ann burst out in laughter. "You did not just say that!"

He shrugged, "Are you telling me I'm wrong? Are my abilities not all you led me to believe that they were?" He hung his head and slumped down into a chair. "I guess you've been faking all of those orgasms huh?"

She just shook her head at him and smiled. "You are something else you know that? Arrogant, self centered, not to mention *cocky.*"

"Yeah, I am aren't I?" He gave her his best smile and winked. "But that's why you love me." *Shit!* As soon as he said it he knew his mistake. He had only been messing around. Teasing her. But the look on her face spoke volumes of how uncomfortable he'd made her.

"Well, I think I'm all set here. Thanks for helping me with everything. So, I'll see you tonight at home." She walked over and gave him a peck on the cheek before attempting to turn away. But Quinn wouldn't let her.

Quinn grabbed her wrist and held her close to him. "Ann—I…Are you okay?" He could feel her body trembling.

No. I'm not okay at all. "Of course I am. So I'll see you tonight then?"

She was pulling away again. *Damn it! When was this going to end?* He thought about telling her right then and there that he was in love with her. But the uncertainty in her eyes and the trembling of her hands told him that she wasn't ready.

Would she ever be? Quinn silently asked himself the question. *Why did she always do this?* Whenever they would get close, she would shut down and build up these walls around her. He absolutely hated it.

"Babe, did I make you uncomfortable?"

"What? No, no I'm just worried. I've never handled the restaurant all by myself before." She gave him a small smile, in an attempt to reassure him.

She was lying. He knew that she was. "Are you sure? Because you seemed to get a little nervous when I said that—"

"Quinn, please, don't be ridiculous. Really I'm fine. Now don't you have to go?"

If she had a ten foot pole she would have been using it to push him out the door. "Yeah, I guess I do."

Quinn walked toward the back of the restaurant. He could feel her following behind him, just inches away. She drove him crazy with this constant push and pull thing they had going with their relationship. He would push her, and then she would pull away.

Abruptly, Quinn spun around and grabbed her. Picking her up he walked into the office with her.

"Quinn, what are you doing?" She was pushing on his chest in an effort to be put back down. "The chef is gonna be here any minute."

Quinn took what she said and pondered it. So, with her still being held in his arms, feet dangling off of the floor, his large hands cupping her bottom, he kicked the door shut.

"Quinn? What's gotten into you?"

Finally, he set her down and looked at her. He let his gaze wash over her entire body as he took in the sight of the perfection that she was. He lifted his hands and stroked the backs of his fingers down her cheeks. He smiled when she unconsciously closed her eyes and let her lips part open for him.

Quinn brought his lips within a millimeter of hers when he whispered, "*You've* gotten into me baby."

His words, along with the way that he said them sent a hot streak of aching need down to her womb. "Quinn…"

He kissed the tip of her nose and pulled away. "Have a good night honey. Call me if you need anything." Then he walked out.

Ann stood there stunned. The short moment they had just shared had been so intimate, so perfect. And then he'd left. Ann turned and looked at her flushed cheeks in the mirror.

"You'd better get a hold of yourself, Ann."

Chapter Thirteen

Quinn was finishing up payroll at the Roadhouse when Derek walked in his office.

"Hey man what's up," he asked as he barely looked up from his computer screen.

Derek sat in the chair opposite his brother and eyed him speculatively. What could he say, and how could he say it? He cared about them both and knew that Ann was slowly dying inside. It was no secret that she was desperately in love with his brother, except to Quinn. But just three weeks after they first met and she was more convinced than ever that Quinn would soon be breaking her heart.

Oh sure, she tried to stay strong and act like nothing was bothering her. But every so often at the restaurant he would catch her staring off, and he could see the fear in her eyes. He tried to talk to her, reassure her. But no matter how much he did, she still believed that she wasn't enough to make Quinn happy. At least not for long. He wished she didn't have such a low opinion of herself. He wished that she could see all the beauty and wonder that he did in her.

It was crazy really, seeing as how he grew up with the little shit. He laughed.

"What's so funny?" Quinn wondered.

Derek expelled a breath before speaking. "You see, here's the deal. Well, you're my brother and all so I'm kind of like forced to love you and care about you and all that other crap right?"

Quinn stopped typing and looked up at him confused. "Come again?"

Oh hell. "Look I know you haven't had the best of luck with relationships, you know, because of your problem."

Now Quinn was really getting worried. "Yeah? What is it? Is it Ann?"

Derek nodded, "Yeah."

Shit! "What is it? Is she hurt?" Quinn got up from his chair and headed for the door. "Where is she?"

Derek outstretched his leg to stop him. "Hold on there, partner. She's fine." Derek motioned for him to return to his chair and waited for him to do just that.

Quinn sat back down and eyed his brother with animosity. "What the hell is it then?"

Shit. I do not want to do this. I don't want to get involved. "How do you feel about her?"

Quinn just bunched his brows together. What exactly was he asking? "Why? Is someone…did someone hit on her?"

"No. No, it's just that. Well, she's been sort of distracted lately. Have you noticed that?"

Actually, he had. Ever since he asked her to move in she had become increasingly distant. Only sporadically, but he had still noticed it. It was like one moment she was happy and fun to be around and the next she would withdraw from him and seem so sad. And it was almost always followed up with a passionate bout of sex.

"Well, have you?" Derek asked again.

"Yeah, I guess distracted is one way to put it." Quinn didn't want to admit it but at first he had just written it off to the emotional crap women go through. But lately he had been in denial. He didn't want to admit that she might not be that happy. His love for her had only gotten stronger and he didn't want to lose her.

"Well?" God, it was like talking to a freaking dog.

"Well, what?" Now Quinn was getting pissed. What the hell business was it of his brothers anyway? This was between him and Ann.

"Jesus, do I have to spell it out for you? Damn man, don't you know what's bothering her?"

Actually no, he almost said. But the idea that Derek knew what was upsetting her and he didn't just pissed him off even more. "This is none of your damn business!" Quinn shouted.

Derek was surprised by Quinn's reaction. He normally didn't have much of a temper. But if getting his temper fired up was what it was going to take to get Ann back to normal, then so be it.

"Look. I'm not trying to be an asshole here."

"Then why are you being one?"

Shit. "Geez man. Chill. I ah…care about Ann. And I—" Derek wasn't able to finish his speech because the next thing he knew, he felt the swift blow to the side his jaw. Derek went down. Tumbling backwards in his chair.

"Are you fucking kidding me? You're my fucking brother!" Quinn shouted at him.

Derek looked up from the floor, stunned for a moment. Then realization struck him and he realized what Quinn had thought.

"How could you? Is that why she's been so distant?" Quinn started pacing.

Derek got up from the floor. "Quinn, let me explain."

Quinn spun around to face him. "Explain! How the fuck could you?" He then let out a tortured laugh. "I should have known. It was too damn good to be true. Women never enjoyed having sex with me." He turned to face his brother. "So what, you're better in bed then?"

Derek stood there dumbfounded. How could they have gone from him coming here to counsel his brother on freaking relationship advice to him thinking he was screwing Ann? "Quinn, listen to me damn it!"

"No you fucking listen! You're dead to me. Do you hear me? D-E-A-D." Quinn said nothing more as he stormed out of his office.

What in the fuck just happened? "Quinn, wait!" Derek shouted after him.

Derek got into the parking lot just in time to see Quinn's truck speeding off into the distance. *Holy Hell! What had he done?* Worse, what the hell had his brother done? Derek ran to his truck, knowing he had to catch up with Quinn before he did something stupid.

Derek reached into his pocket for his cell phone so that he could call Ann and warn her. He hadn't even told Ann that he had been planning on talking to his brother. But now he was going to have to warn her that not only had he done what she had explicitly asked him not to, but he was also going to have to explain how he had royally fucked things up for her. *Shit! Shit! Shit!*

Quinn was speeding down the dirt road. He took one of the turns way too fast but he didn't care. He loved her. How could she do this to him, to them? He knew she had been distant lately, but he also knew how good things could be between them. Had she been faking her happiness, among other things? Was her happiness only for Derek?

Fucking Derek! He could kill him right now. They were brothers. They knew all too well from their upbringing what sharing someone could do to a family. He almost had to laugh at the similarities of their current situation and that with which they were raised in.

He was forced to stop thinking about it when he heard a phone ringing. It wasn't his though, it was Ann's. He reached down in the console and found it. She must have left it in his truck yesterday. He looked at the screen and cringed when he saw it was Derek calling. He answered.

"You fucking dick! Is it not enough you stole her from me? You have to call her? And right after you tell me, no less?" Quinn slammed the phone shut, effectively disconnecting the call.

"Quinn—" That was the only word Derek was able to get out before Quinn hung up. Could things possibly get any worse? As if Murphy himself, the infamous law man, had swooped down and cast his shadow over Derek's truck, he heard the sirens as they started to wail. He looked in his rearview mirror and saw none other than Deputy O'Reily. The same asshole that had had it in for him since freaking high school ever since Mary Sue Gallagher gave him her virginity instead of O'Reily. Granted he dated Mary Sue for two years, so it should have been his place to take her, but she wanted Derek. *What was he supposed to do, say no? Well, I guess that answers that question,* Derek muttered to himself. Things just got a lot worse.

Ann was washing dishes and loading them into the dishwasher when she heard the screeching tires in the driveway. She instantly dried her hands and raced to the front door. But it opened before she got there and in stomped Quinn. Full of raging fury.

"Quinn, hi…what are you doing home? I thought you had to—"

"Shut up!" He shouted at her.

Ann's mouth flew open in surprise. He had never spoken to her so rudely before. "What's wrong? Are you upset?"

He let out a guttural laugh then looked at her. "Upset? No. God, no. Why would I be upset? I mean hell, it's not like you and my brother have been keeping fucking secrets from me or anything." *There! Stew over that!*

"Secrets? Quinn what are you—" She was confused by his accusation.

This time Quinn really did laugh. "Oh, so he didn't tell you he was going to tell me. Well, I guess the jokes on you now, because I know." When she looked down he stalked over to her and raised her chin to meet his steely gaze. "I know everything!"

No! Derek swore he wouldn't say anything. *Why didn't he believe her?* She had known that if Quinn knew about her true feelings she would lose him. And now he knew. He knew she was in love with him and her worst fears were coming true. They hadn't talked about commitment. And it was more than obvious from his reaction to the news that he didn't want one either.

Ann blinked back the tears. "Quinn, please. I'm…wait, no. I'm not going to say I'm sorry, because I'm not."

If she had hit him with a two by four, Quinn couldn't have been knocked more off balance as he was at that moment. He figured she would cry. He even figured she would try to deny it. Maybe even beg him for another chance. But to hear her stand there and say that she wasn't even sorry. *How dare she!* He had given her everything that was his, including his soul. He loved her more than anything. He silently thanked himself for never giving into his need to tell her his true feelings.

"Quinn, don't just look at me like that. Say something."

"Say something? What in the fuck do you propose that I say?"

This time the tears did come. "I don't know. I just…Quinn, everything that Derek said was true. And I can't change how I feel. When you love someone, it just is. You can't turn it off."

His shock had intensified. She was in love with Derek? "You bitch! Get out of my house! Now!"

Ann felt his fury. The anger in his voice reverberated with every word that he spoke. "Quinn…please." She was down-right sobbing now and she didn't care. She loved him. She actually let herself believe that he cared for her and that maybe one day he might even love her as much as she loved him. How could she have been so wrong? Did the thought of her loving him disgust him so much?

Quinn had started to walk away when he heard her plea. "You stupid, ignorant bitch. You expect me to be okay with this? You disgust me!" And with that he slammed the bedroom door.

Ann fell to the floor. She was crying so hard her entire body was shaking. Eight weeks. She had had eight weeks with him. It wasn't enough. She knew it. She knew he could never love her. He was too handsome, too smart and too damn sexy. There were plenty of women out there that could probably offer him much more than she ever could. She was a hostess in a restaurant for Christ sakes. She was nothing.

Quinn listened to her tears on the other side of the door. *What right did she have to cry,* he thought? *What right did she have to feel any amount of pain?* He was the one that was hurting, he was in pain. He stayed there, leaning against the door and listened to her sobs. *Why was she still crying?* He couldn't stand it any longer. When he blinked, a tear escaped and trailed down his face. *Stop crying*, he silently told her. It was killing him to hear her cry.

Quinn squeezed his eyes shut to stop the flow of tears. "Baby, please don't cry," he whispered. But she didn't hear him and she didn't stop. Quinn fought everything inside of him to keep from going to her. He shouldn't care. He should hate her, despise her. But he didn't. He loved her. *God damn it. He loved her so damn much.*

Finally, Ann had stopped. Quinn looked at his watch. Forty five minutes. She had cried for forty five minutes and he had stood there and did nothing. He could hear her moving around. What was she doing? Then he heard her keys. She was leaving. *No, don't go,* he wanted to shout to her. But he knew he couldn't. She was quiet again; then he almost jumped out of his skin at the sound of her voice on the other side of the door.

"Quinn." Her voice was barely audible. She sounded hoarse and sickly. "I'm leaving. I'll come back tonight to…get my things." She sniffled.

Was she crying again? *Annie, please don't cry.*

"I just wanted you to know that, well I…I meant what I said, about how I felt. I love—" She was interrupted by the sound of more tires screeching in the driveway. She ran to the door and opened it. Derek.

"Ann, thank God. You didn't have your phone with you. I've been trying to call you." He had been so frantic while he dealt with that dick O'Reily, who set the world record on how long it takes to write a damn speeding ticket. "I talked to Quinn and—"

Whap! Ann slapped him with every amount of pain that she felt. His stupid meddling had caused this. "I hate you! How could you tell him? You swore to me you'd never tell." She didn't wait for an answer. She just ran to her car and sped away.

Derek rubbed his cheek. *Fuck. Shit. Damn.* They weren't the most creative words. But they adequately described the clusterfuck that this afternoon had turned into. He could have gone after her, but he knew that it would make no difference. Until he cleared things up with Quinn, nothing was going to get fixed.

So he took a deep breath and walked in the house. He closed the door and looked up to see his brother standing there, tears streaked down his face. "Oh shit. You've been crying."

Quinn wanted to rage at his brother, he wanted to tear him to shreds. But he knew it would do no good. If Ann had really cared for him, she wouldn't have cheated on him. He turned from his brother and went to the kitchen.

Derek followed him, "Quinn, you need to listen to me."

Quinn ignored him, reaching for his bottle of Jack Daniels and a shot glass. "Go to hell."

"Quinn, you're wrong. I never slept with her." There. If he wouldn't let him explain he would just have to let little pieces of the truth spill out into the conversation.

Quinn turned and looked at him. It helped a little to hear it, but it didn't much matter. Because while he was in love with her, she was in love with Derek.

"I guess I should thank you, but I'm not feeling too cordial right now. Seeing as how she's in love with you and all."

This time it was Derek's turn to be shocked. "What?"

"You gonna make me repeat that?" Quinn screamed the question.

"Wait. This doesn't make any sense. Why on earth do you think she's in love with me?" *What in the hell was going on?*

Quinn turned to face his brother. With new tears escaping his eyes he said, "She told me."

Derek shook his head in bewilderment. "What?" He knew for a fact that Ann was desperately and hopelessly in love with Quinn.

Why on earth would she have told Quinn that she was in love with him? But within that question was his answer. She wouldn't have. No way would Ann have told him that.

"What exactly did she say?" Derek demanded.

Quinn looked at his brother, seriously reconsidering his position on murder. "I can't believe you're going to make me go over this again."

Derek reached into Quinn's refrigerator and pulled out two beers, handing one to his brother he said, "Yeah, well I am gonna. Because I might have screwed up today, but I have a feeling you did too. So sit down, drink your beer and tell me everything she said."

Quinn sat in the chair opposite his brother and popped off the lid. Taking a big swig, he glared at his brother. "She said she couldn't turn her feelings of love off. She said that when you love someone it just is. Or something like that. Fuck, I hate you!"

Derek took the verbal attack in stride. Because in a matter of minutes he knew that Quinn would be looking at himself in the mirror and uttering those same words. "She said when you love 'someone'?"

"Yeah." *Why was he even sitting here talking to his asshole of a brother?*

"So, at what point in your educational background did you start mixing up the word 'someone' with 'Derek'? Just wondering, because the 'someone' she's in love with is you." *There. Put that in your pipe and smoke it you hot-headed jerk.*

Quinn set down his beer and stared at his brother. "What?"

Derek nodded. "That's what I went there to tell you. She and I have become good friends working at the restaurant together." Derek held up his hand to shut him up. "She confided in me. She's been in love with you almost since the beginning. But she always had this paranoid delusion that you would get tired of her. She lived everyday in fear that you were going to dump her for someone else."

"What?" He couldn't believe what he was hearing.

"I know. Look, you know she's only had two boyfriends. Not a lot of experience for someone her age. She's still young, at heart I mean. She assumed that if she cared about you too much, or showed you how she felt, that you would go running for the hills. After you kicked her out, of course."

"But, I…I told her you came to see me. I told her that I knew everything. She didn't deny it, she accepted that I knew." This didn't make any sense.

"Right. She thinks I told you that she was in love with you. And that she was afraid to lose you." Derek watched the horror creep across his brother's face when realization had hit.

"No! Oh shit! Derek, I was horrible to her. I called her a bitch. Oh fuck. What have I done? Where did she go? Do you know where she might have gone? I have to find her." Quinn was already getting up from the table.

"Hang on. There's something else you have to know."

Quinn stopped in his tracks. "What?"

Derek took a breath, knowing that this might be more shocking than everything else. "I think Ann's pregnant."

Quinn dropped into the chair in disbelief. He shook his head for several minutes with his mouth hanging open, and then slowly turned to his brother.

"So, if I understand you right, the woman that I love, the only woman that I've ever loved, is pregnant with my child. She loves me, so much that she is riddled with anxiety over whether I'll leave her." Quinn took a breath. "And to help her through these things that she's going through I scream at her, call her a bitch and tell her to get out."

Derek shook his head. "Yeah man, that pretty much covers it."

"Holy hell. What in the hell is wrong with me?" Quinn dropped his forehead to the table. Too much shocking information all at once was not good for the soul.

Chapter Fourteen

Ann didn't know where she was. She just drove and drove until she was lost. She kept replaying everything that happened when Quinn had gotten home. She couldn't believe the cruel words he had used when he found out she loved him. He called her a bitch. He knew how much she hated when men called women that. Did the idea of her loving him make him so angry that he would want nothing but to hurt her?

She saw a small hotel on the side of the road and pulled off to see if they had any vacancies. She knew she had told Quinn she would be back tonight for her things, but there was no way she could go back there tonight. She was tired, her head hurt and the pain she felt in her chest was unbearable. Maybe she would go back tomorrow night.

She got out of her car and headed for the front office. There was an old man behind the counter and he turned away from his television to face her when she entered. He gave her a concerned smile. She knew she probably looked like hell.

"Do you have any rooms available?"

"Are you all right, Miss?"

It was then that Ann saw her reflection in the window. She looked worse than hell. There were mascara streaks staining her face. Her eyes were beyond puffy and swollen. She actually looked like she'd been punched in the eyes.

"I'm fine. Thank you though. Do you, have a room I mean?"

"Sure. Ah, do you need to talk to someone? I could get my wife. She's in the back fixing us supper."

Ann smiled at the sweet man and his kindness. “No, thank you really. I just want a bed and a hot bath. And maybe some dinner. Are there any restaurants around here?”

He shook his head. “Do you like spaghetti and meatballs?”

“Yes, actually I do.”

He reached up and handed her a pen and a paper. “Fill this out. We’ll need to see an ID and a credit card, but you can pay cash if you want when you check out.” He leaned closer to her and whispered, even though there was no one else in the room. “The wife gets a little pissed when people leave without paying. So we started taking down card numbers.”

She nodded. “I understand.”

“Okay well, you fill all that out and I’ll be right back.” He disappeared into the backroom.

Ann filled out the registration card and hesitated when it asked for her address. It made her sad. She just went to the bank yesterday and ordered some checks with Quinn’s address on them. She told herself she was being silly, but she had a bad feeling that she was jinxing herself.

Ann had just dotted the last I and crossed the last T when the sweet old man came back out from the back room. She couldn’t contain her grin when she saw the food he was holding. And following behind him was a lady much larger than him. It almost shocked her for a moment. He was probably only 5 feet tops and she was easily 5 1/2 feet and had packed on a few pounds more than her husband over the years.

“Is this her? Oh my dear, look at you. You just look dreadful.”

The man nudged his wife. “That’s not making her feel better.”

“Of course. I’m sorry dear. Is it a man? Is that what has upset you so?”

“I told you she said she doesn’t want to talk about it,” he told his wife.

“It’s fine, and thank you for the food. I assume that’s for me.”

"Indeed. Listen I'm Marilyn Bates and this here is my husband. No—" He quickly interrupted her.

"Let's just leave her be," He told her, giving her an evil eye.

Marilyn rolled her eyes. "Oh for heaven's sake. Would you get over it already? It's not that big of a deal."

Ann was curious. "What's not that big of deal?"

"His name," she said, "It's Norman, Norman Bates."

Ann couldn't help it. She burst out laughing. "Norman Bates? Are you serious?"

He nodded up at her. "I'm afraid so. If you notice the sign outside just says Motel. We thought The Bates Motel would be bad for business."

Ann kept laughing. "Oh my God. I can imagine the people in the city and county office when you applied for your business license." She laughed harder.

Her laughter was contagious because now they were all laughing. In a funny voice Ann continued, "So, Mr. Bates, it says here you would like to run a roadside motel. Will that be with or without the dead bodies?"

Their laughter continued into the night as she ended up staying and eating dinner with the fun couple. She went to her room to wash up first, but had gone right back to join them for one of the best spaghetti and meatball dinners she had ever eaten.

It was now 8 o'clock. She knew Quinn would be at the Roadhouse. It would be safe to go back and get her things now without having to hear anymore of his hurtful words, but she didn't want to go back yet. The Bates' had given her directions to get back to the main highway, so she could go whenever she wanted to. The only problem was that all she really wanted was Quinn. Despite everything he had said and how much he had hurt her, she still loved him. And she knew it wasn't going to be easy getting over him. Actually, if she was completely honest with herself, she knew she wouldn't ever be able to get over him. She would love him forever.

Ann tuned on the water to the bathtub when she realized that she didn't even have a cell phone. That, of course, made her realize that she had absolutely no one to call. No one to reassure that she was all right and safe. She knew Derek would probably be worried about her. But she didn't really care. She was furious with him for meddling in something that he swore to keep a secret. Sure, it was Quinn that had actually hurt her. But if Derek hadn't have stuck his stupid nose in their business she would still be there right now.

So what if he didn't love her. She could be happy without his love, as long as she had him. She shook her head as she dipped her body slowly into the bath. That wasn't true and she knew it. She did love Quinn, but she needed his love, too. That's what all her nervousness had been about. She needed him, all of him. All or nothing.

Like it matters now, she thought. It was over, he didn't love her and that was that. She laid her head back against the tub and closed her eyes, wishing she could change it from happening. A stray lonely tear slid down her cheek. She already missed him so much. *Oh Quinn, I love you.*

* * * *

Quinn paced the living room. He hated that he wasn't out there helping Derek look for her. But he couldn't take the chance that she would come home and he wasn't there. He could leave a note. But there was no way that he could possibly put down on paper the turmoil that he was experiencing right now. She was out there somewhere, pregnant, hurting, and probably crying her eyes out and it was all his fault. And he knew it. The phone finally rang and he jumped for it.

"Hello, Annie?"

Derek sighed on the other end. "No bro, sorry. It's me. I was just checking in. Any word yet?"

"No, damn it. Where could she be?"

Derek knew that Quinn was aware he didn't have the answers. But the whole situation was just so frustrating. He had already apologized to Quinn earlier for causing all of this. But Quinn wouldn't let him take the blame.

Quinn hated what had happened. He knew that if he had only listened to Derek, or if he had only trusted Ann, then none of this would have happened. And he knew that was the worst part about it.

"Derek, did you check the hotel?"

"Yeah. I don't know where else to look man, I'm sorry. I haven't seen her car and no one's seen her either."

Quinn fought the knot in his stomach. What if she was really gone? Like for good. "Derek, you said you two have talked, that you're friends right?"

"Yeah, why? What are you thinking?"

Quinn could barely say the words, scared that saying them would make them true. "You don't think she left for good do you? I mean, she'll be back right?"

Derek listened to his brother's tortured voice. The truth was that about an hour ago Derek had wondered the exact same thing. But he didn't want to worry Quinn anymore than he already was. "Her clothes are there, she left with nothing but her purse. Where could she go?" But as soon as Derek said it, he knew he shouldn't have.

"She's been working, she has no bills. She's saved up money. Oh God." Quinn sat down on the couch in his living room. "What if she really left me?"

Derek hated to hear the pain in his brother's voice. "You can't think like that, Quinn. She'll be back. She loves you."

Quinn hoped to hell that he was right. But he knew there was a chance, and a big one, that she wouldn't be back. He had seen to that by treating her so badly and using the words he did, just to hurt her. "Just keep looking. Please."

"Sure man, call me if you hear from her, okay?" Derek hung up and turned his truck around, preparing to make another run around town.

Quinn set his phone down. He was numb. He kept replaying their argument earlier. He remembered, just like she was standing before him, the pain in her eyes. The pleading in her voice when she tried to explain things to him. When she had tried to tell him that she loved him. That she couldn't help it, because it just was.

"Oh God." He loved her and he hurt her. He could almost hear her gut wrenching cries echoing through the house. He caused her such pain. How could he have done that to her? And the baby. Dear God, the baby. She was pregnant. She shouldn't be upset.

"Please come home, Annie." He said aloud to no one but an empty room. "Please, just come home."

* * * *

Ann got out of the tub and dried herself off. Marilyn had been kind enough to lend her one of her night shirts. It was huge on her, but the cotton was soft and felt soothing against her now clean skin. She applied lotion from the little mini bottle that the hotel provided and ran the tiny black comb, also provided by the hotel, through her hair. It took forever to finally get it all combed and tangle free, but finally she was ready for bed.

She wondered how she could even think to sleep in a bed without Quinn ever again. She loved the warmth of his body as he held her close. And when he would make love to her, it was so amazing. She wished she was with him now. She wished this horrible day had never happened. But what she really wished was that he would love her, just as she did him.

Lying in bed, she curled on her side. Instinctively, almost out of habit she reached her hand over to lay it on Quinn's chest. It was a habit that she had become accustomed to every night. She saw the phone and willed it to ring. Wishing upon every star in the sky that Quinn would call and tell her it had all been a lie. That he didn't mean those things and that he loved her.

She closed her eyes and tried to keep the tears at bay. "I love you, Quinn." She whispered the words before she drifted off to sleep.

* * * *

Quinn awoke to the smell of coffee brewing in is kitchen. He jumped from the couch and ran into the kitchen. His anticipation quickly turned to disappointment, because he only saw Derek standing there.

"Sorry, man. I didn't mean to wake you."

Quinn stalked over to the cabinet that held the coffee mugs. "You shouldn't have let me sleep at all."

Derek shook his head. "What can you do? All you can do now is wait."

"I want to be awake if she comes home. I don't want her to think I'm sleeping like a baby when she's been off somewhere hurting," Quinn pointed out.

Derek nodded his agreement. "Listen, I need your keys to the Roadhouse. A couple of your employees called last night. They need their paychecks."

"Oh shit." Quinn turned to face him. "I forgot. Yesterday was payday. I was so upset by, well by what I thought, and I just totally forgot about them. Damn!"

"Don't worry about it, man. Love does crazy things to people. Just give me your keys and I'll take care of them."

Quinn grabbed the Roadhouse keys off of the kitchen hook and tossed them Derek's way. "Thanks. Look, give them something a little extra. Their job isn't easy with the clientele we get, the least I could do is pay them on time."

"Sure, I'll throw in a couple of dinners at the restaurant, too." And Derek walked out, leaving Quinn alone.

Quinn sat there and drank his coffee. He glanced over and saw his Stetson on the hook behind the door. Ann loved it when he wore that hat. He would wear it every day, every minute, every second if she would just come back. He would do anything to make up to her what he did. The things he said he could never take back. But he would apologize until the day that he died for hurting her.

And their baby. He never thought much about having children. But knowing that she was carrying his was causing this ache in his chest. It was a good ache. Like an ache that embraces you and holds on so tightly while it loves you senseless. He took a couple more swigs of his coffee and headed back to the bedroom. He needed a shower and a shave. He couldn't look like hell when she came home. Because she had to come home, the alternative was something he could not fathom.

* * * *

Ann woke up with a killer headache, which she expected from all of the tears. It still sucked because on top of losing the man that she loved, having to go to the home that she was sharing with him and move out, now she had to deal with the onset of a migraine.

She got dressed in yesterday's clothes and picked up the room the best she could. Marilyn and Norman had been so nice and generous she couldn't bear the idea of her leaving them a mess to clean up. She closed the door and headed to the lobby to check out. But when she got there, the door was locked. She was about to knock when she looked up and saw a note taped to the inside window:

Dearest Ann,

We're not here to see you off. Which means we aren't there to collect your room fee either, OOPS!

I guess we goofed.

Seriously though, dear. You are a sweetheart and it is obvious that you needed a safe and quiet place to be alone with your thoughts last night, so I hope you found that here.

Take care of yourself and don't take no crap from that man that has you so worked into a tizzy!

Good Luck,

Marilyn & Norman

P.S. See, you didn't get killed in the shower or see any dead bodies.

Chapter Fifteen

It was after five o'clock, and Quinn was getting more scared as the minutes ticked by. He should have already been at the Roadhouse by then, getting ready for their busy Saturday night. But he wasn't leaving. Ann knew that he was supposed to be there and that was what was killing him. *Was the fact that she hadn't come home yet a sign that she wasn't come back at all?* He would have continued to ponder that if he hadn't heard her key hit the lock.

Quinn jumped up and made his way to the door. He didn't get there in time to open it, because now she stood in the doorway, facing him. Her face was covered in shock and she turned white as a sheet as she stared at him.

"Quinn, I…I'm…" She burst into tears and turned away. She obviously hadn't expected to see him there. She started to walk back outside when his arms encircled her and held her tightly against him.

"Please don't go, baby."

Ann swallowed the lump in her throat and leaned against him. "What do you want?" She asked him, the fear evident in her voice.

"I'm sorry, Annie. God, I'm so sorry. Please let me explain. Don't go, just stay and let me explain."

Ann listened as he whispered in her ear. His voice was strained. She turned her head to look up at him and saw that he had been crying? "Quinn, are you okay?"

That was it. He couldn't hold back anymore. He hurt her horribly and she was so good and so caring that she was worried about him. He swung her around to face him and before he could give her a chance to pull away he held onto her in an embrace that was pure possession.

"I'm so sorry, honey." Quinn whispered in her ear. "Please forgive me."

She started to cry and looked confused. She pulled back, but only slightly to look up at him. "What…why did…I thought…I don't understand."

Quinn placed a gentle kiss to her forehead and lingered there. "I know, honey. I know how confused you must be. I screwed up bad. Come inside. I'll explain everything. Just please come inside and sit down with me."

Ann didn't answer as she walked past him and into the house. She sat nervously on the couch. Her expression was one of wonder and confusion. He hated that he was the reason that she looked that way.

Quinn sat next to her. He picked up her hand and laced their fingers together. "I'm sorry, Annie. I didn't mean any of the horrible things that I said to you." He hesitated for a moment. "I love you."

Her mouth dropped open in shock. He knew she was in disbelief of what he'd just said. The cute, dazed look in her eyes also told him that she was lost in her thoughts. He was about to say it again when she started to speak.

"Did you just say that you love me?"

Quinn released his hand from hers and brought his hands up to frame the sides of her face, gently caressing her cheeks with his thumbs. "I did. I love you. I love you so damn much, Annie. I was lost last night when I thought you weren't coming back."

Ann listened to him intently. He was still talking, but she seemed to have drifted off to some far recess of her mind. As if analyzing everything before responding. "You really love me?"

She began to cry, but he quickly nodded to her, indicating that he did. He really did love her. "Oh Quinn. I love you so much. I've been so afraid to tell you."

Quinn hated her tears, and wished he wasn't the cause of her pain. "I know, and I'm sorry for everything that I said to you yesterday. Please believe me, I'll do whatever it takes, if you'd give me another chance."

Ann leaned into him and buried herself against his solid chest. "Anything. I'll do anything for you Quinn." She looked up at him. "You really love me?"

He hated the doubt he saw in her eyes. "I swear I do, honey. Please don't doubt that. I love you."

She shook her head, confused. "But why did you get so angry with me when you found out that I loved you? You acted like you…" She couldn't finish the words. It was too painful to remember the hatred she saw in his eyes.

"I acted like an asshole. That's what I acted like, and I'm so sorry." He held her closer to him. Needing to feel the sweetness of her body snuggled against his.

"You acted like you hated me. Why?" She shouldn't ask, she should just be happy that they were together and that he loved her. But she needed to know.

Quinn closed his eyes and relished in the feel of her warm body. "I didn't think you were in love with me. I thought it was Derek. I thought you were in love with him."

That got her attention. She pulled away and stared at him. "Derek? Why on earth did you think that?"

"I sensed your distance and sadness. I knew something was going on. I tried to talk to you, but you would never tell me what was bothering you." He took a breath and took her hands in his. "Derek was getting worried about you. He wanted to tell me how important it was that I get off of my ass and tell you how I really feel about you. He said that you were feeling insecure."

Ann dropped her head, not wanting to look him in the eye and admit to him how she had lived in fear for the past two months thinking he could never love her. "I thought that you would get tired of me. I fell for you so hard, so fast. I fell in love with you in under a week." She laughed at the ridiculousness of her statement, but continued more seriously, "I didn't think that I could make you happy."

"Do you know how crazy that is? I've been in love with you this whole time. But I've been holding back, I didn't want to scare you away." They both laughed a little. "We're quite the pair, aren't we?"

"I still don't see why you thought I fell in love with Derek," she wondered, needing to have all of her questions answered.

He was going to have to tell her all of it, he just hated that they were going to have to relive that pain. "When Derek was trying to tell me that you were upset and he knew why, he was trying to help me, help us. But all I heard was that he knew what was bothering you. That you had confided in him and not me. And that cut deep, but not as deep as why I thought you had confided in him. I figured, why I don't know, that you confided in him because you had developed feelings for each other."

Quinn shook his head. Hearing himself say it aloud now sounded so ridiculous. If only he had stopped to think yesterday, he would have known that Annie never would have done that to him. Not to mention his brother.

"Quinn, that's crazy."

"I know that now, but see when he was trying to talk to me I wasn't listening. Somehow I got the impression that he was trying to tell me that you two were together and that I was out of the picture."

She still didn't understand. *How could he think that*? "But when you came home, I told you that I loved you."

"No, honey. You told me that you loved someone and that you weren't sorry for it because you couldn't turn off your feelings." He pulled her closer and brought his mouth within inches of hers. "I thought you were trying to tell me that it was Derek that you loved. My heart broke when I thought you loved someone else. So I lashed out. I was angry and hurt. That's why I said those things. But I swear to you I didn't mean any of them, honey. Please believe that I would do anything to take away the pain that I caused you yesterday."

Ann brought her lips the final distance to meet with his. Kissing him, she tried to not cry at the joy she was feeling . "I love you, Quinn. I could never love anyone else. You're everything to me." This time she did cry, overcome with raw emotion.

"Annie, don't cry. Honey, please." Quinn began to kiss her tear streaked cheeks. "Baby, you have no idea how much it hurt me to hear you cry yesterday. I wanted to go to you and hold you. But I was hurt too, and I couldn't. My pride wouldn't let me."

"Just hold me. Hold me and don't let me go."

Quinn did just that. He held her tight against his body and rocked her. He didn't want to stop, but he knew that he had to call Derek. "Honey I have to call Derek. He was worried about you too."

"Oh God, Derek. I slapped him, hard. I have to apologize to him."

Quinn just shook his head. "No, it was mine and Derek's fault. We are both at fault for what happened yesterday, you did nothing but get hurt. But never again. If you give me another chance, I promise I will never hurt you again."

She smiled at him. Her first genuine smile of over twenty four hours. "Of course I'll give you another chance. Quinn, I love you. I prayed for this last night. I went to bed and wished that you would love me and want me."

"Damn, I'm so lucky. Thank you, Annie."

"Thank you? For what?"

"For everything. For giving me another chance that day in my office," he winked at her, "for loving me." He placed his hand to her stomach and said, "and for our baby."

Her smile quickly left her face. *Why did he think she was pregnant?* "Baby? Quinn, I'm not pregnant."

"Honey, it's okay. Derek told me," he assured her.

She looked at him confused. "He told you what exactly?"

Quinn cocked his head at her, wishing she would trust him enough to tell him and be as happy as he was. "He told me about the test he found in the employee bathroom trash at work. It's okay, honey. I'm so happy. We'll be fine. I'll take care of you."

She pulled back further from him, needing him to see the seriousness on her face. "Quinn, listen to me. I am *not* pregnant."

He shook his head. "But the test that Derek found said it was positive."

"Quinn, I am one of six women that work at the restaurant. Someone may be pregnant. But it isn't me." She said the words slowly, making sure he heard every word. "You know that I'm on birth control."

Quinn listened to everything that she said. "So, basically I have gotten everything wrong for the past twenty four hours. Right?"

She smiled at him. "Yes. That is right. Because I love you, not Derek, and I am definitely not pregnant."

"Oh God. I'm sorry, honey." He laughed. "I wasn't upset though, I was happy. I would love to have children with you." He realized what he said and the look in her eyes spoke volumes of uncertainty.

"What are you saying, Quinn?"

"I was thinking that you'd do a big asshole an even bigger favor and make him the happiest son of a bitch in the world and marry him." He was going for humor, but could tell that she didn't see it.

"Smooth, real romantic." She was laughing at him. "You should write romantic greeting cards. You'd make a killing." That made her laugh even harder. "Oh, I can't believe I forgot to tell you. I stayed at this little motel about five miles off of route 9 and met the sweetest couple who owned it."

He waited for the funny part. "And?"

"His name was Norman Bates, seriously, it was Norman Bates and he ran a little Motel, just off of the highway."

Quinn looked at her and chuckled. "Should I be worried?"

"No, I was smart. I ate spaghetti with them, you know make friends with the homicidal killers, so they won't want to add you to their victim list. But then I took a bath instead of a shower. Probably messed with their whole routine."

They were both laughing now as the phone rang. Quinn reached for it and saw that it was Derek. He flipped it open and didn't even get a chance to say hello because Derek shouted into his ear.

"Ann's not pregnant," Derek confessed.

"I know. She was more than a little surprised to hear the news. Especially seeing as how the test wasn't hers." Quinn traced his finger along Ann's cheek while he listened to his brother.

"I found that out when I got into work. There was a note from Claire, requesting maternity leave for later this year. Dude, I'm sorry. I guess when I screw with your life, I do it right good."

Quinn laughed. "That you do."

"So, I guess since you're laughing that means everything is going good."

Quinn smiled at her again, unable to hide his giddiness. "Yes, the woman should be sainted. She has graciously decided to let me grovel at her feet and beg her forgiveness for the rest of my life."

Ann tried to reach for the phone. "That's not true." She shouted for Derek to hear. "I love him, and you know it. That's the only thing that saved him."

"Gotta go now, bye." Quinn hung up the phone and kissed her with all of the pent of desire he had felt since he found out that she really did love him, and not his brother.

He laid her back on the couch, he wanted her so bad. He needed to feel her underneath him, writhing against him. "I need you, honey." He reached his hand down to cup her heat through her jeans. "I almost died when I thought I lost you, my heart stopped beating."

She wanted him just as much. She needed to feel his body stroking in and out of hers as they loved one another. "Take me, Quinn. Make me yours in every way that matters."

"You are mine, honey. Oh Annie, and I'm yours. I love you so much." He was on fire for her. His blood was pulsing and pounding straight to his cock. He was so hard he was sure he would die if he wasn't inside of her soon.

Quinn got up from the couch and pulled her to her feet. He kissed her some more and then stopped abruptly. Slowly he dropped to his knees. "Annie, will you please marry me. It doesn't have to be right away. Whenever you want, just say yes. I love you so much and I promise I'll do whatever it takes to make you happy."

She wouldn't cry, she told herself. "Yes," she whispered, "I'll marry you."

Quinn jumped to his feet and swung her around. "We're going to be so happy, honey. I promise."

"Quinn, if you love me, I'll be happy."

"Then you should be ecstatic baby."

She moaned at his tongue sliding from her ear to her neck. "Quinn, please, I need you."

He swept her up in his arms and carried her to the bedroom. Setting her down, he told her, "I am going to make tonight so special for us honey. This is a celebration." He kissed her some more, lingering as he drank in the sweet taste of her kisses.

"How?" She moaned as he started to undress her.

"How what, honey?"

Her head fell back and her eyes were closed. "How are you going to make tonight special? What are we going to do?"

In between nibbles on her neck and ear he answered her. "I'm going to slide into your tight pussy and fuck you just like I know you love it. I want to make you feel so good—what? Why are you looking at me like that honey?"

"What about…I mean I know you have wanted to and I…but we love each other so, wouldn't it be okay?"

What was she talking about? "Honey, what do you mean? What do you want? I'll do anything to make you feel good. You know that."

"I'm not sure it will, feel good I mean, but I've been thinking about it and I want to try it."

It? What was she—*oh, it? Oh Jesus*. "Baby, are you talking about what I think you're talking about?"

Ann was nervous. But she had gone this far, she might as well show him what she had bought two days ago and hidden in the closet. She walked away from him and headed towards the bedroom.

Quinn followed her. He stopped in the doorway when he saw her reach for a bag that was buried on the top shelf. Finally, she retrieved it and set it on the bed. She looked over at him, and he saw the uncertainty in her eyes.

"I drove to Clermont a couple of days ago. The girl at the shop helped me pick out the items she thought we would like based on what I told…well she said these might be good."

Quinn walked over to the bed and glanced at the name of the store emblazoned on the black bag. *Trina's Treats* was apparently a sex toy shop, because Quinn opened the bag and started to take out the contents. In all there were five things. There were three bottles of lubricant, all claiming to have both a warming and a tingling effect and they were also flavored, stating that they were safe for human consumption. Next, he looked at the small finger tip vibrator that looked like he could make very good use of. But none of them looked as erotic as the fifth item. It was a butt plug.

Just the sight of it had his cock hardening more, to the point of being painful. *Did she really want this?* His greatest fantasy and she was going to give it to him? "Are you sure, honey?"

She nodded at him as she unconsciously licked her lips. "I've been curious for a while now. I never thought I could do it, but with you I could. With you I want to. I want to feel all of you, everywhere. I want, and I need to know that there's no part of my body that you haven't made love to."

Quinn needed to be sure; he also needed her to be. "Annie, are you absolutely positive that this is what you want? Tell me exactly what you want me to do. Forget about being shy. Just tell me what you were thinking when you bought these things."

She looked at him, nervous as all hell, and bit on her bottom lip. "I bought them because I want to feel you inside of me there. I want you to fill me there, with all of you." Her words alone were turning her on, not to mention the idea of what they were talking about. "I want you to make love to me in my ass."

Chapter Sixteen

"Come here." Quinn grabbed her and kissed her. *How could he be so lucky?* He had done almost everything wrong, except one thing. He loves her. But the idea that she was going to give him his ultimate fantasy, and that she wanted it too, was turning him on in ways that he hadn't experienced before.

His kisses were wreaking havoc on what little self control she had left. It didn't matter that she was nervous about taking him. Nor did it matter that she couldn't control her body's reaction to the idea of it. She apparently wanted it, she just never knew. Quinn would not hurt her. He vowed this as he watched her and saw her apprehension.

Quinn was going crazy, he had to have her, but he didn't want to rush things. Doing what she wanted, hell what he wanted too, was going to take some tender loving care. It wasn't something he could just rush into, especially with his size. He was considering how he could coax her into being ready for him when she interrupted his thoughts.

"Quinn," she said breathlessly, "can we try…I mean it might hurt a little so…"

"Don't be embarrassed, honey. Tell me what you want." He used a gentle tone to reassure her.

She dropped her head backwards as he began devouring her neck with his lips and tongue. "That pink thing I bought, I thought we could try that first."

He tried not to laugh at how sweet and innocent she could seem one minute, and how voracious she could seem the next. "Honey, do you know what it's called, that pink thing. Do you know exactly what it's used for?"

She wrapped her arms around his head as he continued his assault on her body. She could feel her skin sizzling with every warm swipe of his tongue. She was certain that at any moment she would burst into flames from the heat that he was causing inside of her. "Yeah, I know exactly what it's for. But the name sounds so silly."

Quinn stopped kissing her neck. He framed her face and brought their foreheads to rest against one another. "But it's not silly, baby. It's called a butt plug, and its main purpose is to give you pleasure. That's what I want. I want to make you feel so good."

She was startled when Quinn swung her around. He molded her body against his and ground his hips against the body part in question. She moaned. She still couldn't believe how much she wanted him there, deeply inside of her, loving her in the most intimate way. She reached up around her head and grabbed onto the back of his neck as she rubbed her bottom against his hardness. "Quinn," she whispered his name, in part plea, part invitation.

Quinn understood her request. He reached around and grabbed the hem of her blouse, pulling it over her head and flinging it across the room. He then pushed her away just slightly, so he could reach the clasp to her bra. He unsnapped it and slid the straps down her shoulders and arms. He heard her gasp as he molded his hands to her breasts. He tried not to laugh when he heard her whimper as he brushed his thumbs across her already hard and rigid nipples. He loved how she filled his hands. They were so beautiful and round. The way her areolas would darken when ever her nipples hardened drove him crazy. He wanted to take one in his mouth right now. But there was no way he could tear his cock away from the soft feel of her ass.

Ann was going crazy with this need for him. The idea that he was going to fill her in such a tiny place was making her beyond wet. She could feel her panties were already soaking with her desire. She needed to get undressed and be close to him. She needed to feel his hard muscled body pressed firmly against her softer one. "Quinn, I need you, please."

"Okay, baby. Turn around." He waited for her to face him; his attention was to kiss her. But instead he found himself staring at her. Basking in all of her beauty. "I love you, Annie."

She wanted to smile, but could only barely lift the ends of her mouth. She was overcome with such an intense feeling of peace and of coming home. This was right. Whatever they did, wherever they were, things would be all right as long as they were together. "I love *you,* Quinn. Show me how it can be, love me completely, in every way."

His heart tightened unbearably from her words. As turned on as he was, he had never felt this level of contentment. He was so overwhelmed with emotion that his very soul ached to be closer to her, to make her become his in every single way. He reached down, and without saying anything he began to unsnap her jeans.

Ann fought her swelling emotions from making her eyes close and lose herself in the ecstasy of his touch. But she needed to see him, to look into his eyes.

Quinn removed her jeans and panties. He dropped to his knees as he placed gentle kisses on her stomach. He held her tightly as he laved his tongue all the way from her belly, down to her dark curls. He had to close his eyes as another fantasy, one he had never shared with her, entered his mind. He wondered what she would look like shaved. Unconsciously, he groaned as he kissed her there, wishing he was kissing bare skin.

"Quinn?"

He stopped and looked up at her. "Yeah, honey."

"Have you ever…I…well when I went to that store, the girl there told me something. She must have been able to tell that I'm not very knowledgeable on these things." She hesitated, wishing she was more comfortable with her desires.

Quinn rose to his feet and framed her face, holding her close to him. "Tell me, honey. What did she tell you, what do you want to try?"

Ann bit her bottom lip. "Have you ever wondered what it would be like if I...looked different down there?" The shocked look in his face did nothing to help soothe her nerves. "I shouldn't have said anything, I'm so—"

Quinn kissed her. An animal had broken free inside of him. At the very moment that he was fantasizing about having her bare she had been thinking the exact same thing. And she was so cute when she was nervous, but now he could think of nothing more than lying her down and shaving all of those curly hairs off of her. It would free them from the last barrier separating them.

Pulling back breathlessly, Quinn asked her, "Will you let me do it?"

She was surprised by his question. She thought that he had seemed disgusted by her idea, but not only was he not disgusted, he wanted to do it for her. 'You want to do it? You don't mind?"

He had to laugh at her sweetness. "Oh baby. I have fantasized about what it would be like. How your skin would feel so soft under my tongue." He watched her eyes glitter with desire. "Let me, baby. Let me shave your pussy until it is bare for my touch."

"Yes. Quinn, please." She was lost in him. She needed him to put out the fire that was raging inside of her. "Can we, now?"

Damn she was so sexy when she was aroused. "Yeah honey, go lay down on the bed. I'll be right back." Quinn went into the bathroom and stripped out of his t-shirt and jeans. He opened the medicine cabinet and replaced the blades on the head on his vibrating razor. He then reached into the shower and grabbed her flowery smelling shaving cream that she used on her legs, grabbed a towel and headed back to the bedroom. And there she was. Lying there, so sweet and gorgeous just waiting for him to take her.

"I need you to spread your legs, baby." He had to fight off the urge to bury himself inside of her at the sight. "You'll never know what you do to me. I could never explain what the sight of you does to me."

Ann smiled at him. "I know, you do the same thing to me."

Quinn set down the towel and razor. He sprayed some of the fluffy cream into his hand and set the can back down. He leaned back on his haunches. "Come closer to the edge honey."

Ann did as he told her and waited anxiously. When she first brought up the idea to Quinn, she thought she would have to go in the shower and do it herself. But when he offered to do it for her, she swore she could almost feel an orgasm building inside of her. The girl that she had talked to at the shop had told her that it was an incredible feeling. That being shaved in such a sensitive area was an intense kind of foreplay.

Quinn put the cream on her dark curls. Rubbing it all around and adding more when he didn't have enough to cover every tiny strand. Once she was completely covered he reached over and grabbed the razor. He flipped on the vibrating switch and looked her in the eyes. "Spread your legs further apart, honey. Good. Are you ready?"

She nodded. Even though she was covered with the white cream, she could feel her wetness trickling out of her. She knew from the look in his eyes that he could see her glistening arousal, too.

Quinn leaned over and gently placed the razor at the bottom and swiped it slowly upward. He was stunned when he heard her whimper. He looked up to see that she had grabbed onto her nipples and was squeezing and pinching them. She was like a freaking goddess. "Don't stop doing that, baby."

Ann looked down at him. "You either. Don't stop, Quinn. It felt so—ooh." She didn't get to finish as he ran the vibrating razor against her sensitive skin again.

Quinn continued to slowly and methodically shave every single last hair off of her beautiful pussy. He almost came twice when he watched the wetness pour out of her. She always got wet for him before. But he had never seen such a river flow from her. She was leaving a trail of her wetness down her lips and onto the bed. Quinn just finished with the last tiny curl when he grabbed the towel and wiped her off.

He stared at her. The sight of her bare pussy was more beautiful than he had imagined. Needing to see more of her he reached his fingers to her lips and spread them open. "Oh babe. Damn." He leaned his head down and took her with his mouth. He was so hard for her. He wanted to take her so badly. But the feel of her smooth skin under his lips was like a drug. And her taste. God her sweet taste.

Ann was writhing beneath him. His mouth felt so good. And her skin was so sensitive now. It was as if the tiny hairs had been covering all of her nerve endings, only allowing her to feel some of the pleasure he gave her. But now she felt it all. No matter how good his tongue felt swirling around inside her pussy though, she needed more.

"Quinn, touch me there. Down there, please…I need to feel…something. I feel so empty." Her pleas came out breathless and urgent.

He grabbed onto her hips and brought her closer to the edge of the bed. When she was sitting half on, half off, he brought his hand to her tiny hole. He moaned when he felt that her wetness trickled down to it. Gently and slowly he placed the tip of his forefinger inside. She moaned and surprisingly didn't pull away. He actually felt her scoot closer to him.

Tenderly, Quinn eased his finger in and out of her, each time increasing the pressure. He should be granted a medal of honor, he thought to himself. Because it was taking every damn bit of will power he had to keep from taking her right now. She was urgent for him, writhing and grinding herself further against his mouth and finger. He couldn't wait anymore. As much as he wanted to prolong this for her he had to feel her come. He needed to drink her passion while his finger was still inside her tiny hole. He moved his attention up and away to her clit.

Ann jolted from the sensation. It was twofold. First the overwhelming power that surged through her when he swiped his tongue across her clit, then the feeling of, what, she couldn't describe, but when his finger slid all the way inside of her ass, she almost came. "More…I need more."

Quinn couldn't believe what he was hearing. He was glad that he did though, because he pulled his finger out, dipped his middle finger inside her pussy for more moisture and plunged both fingers inside of her ass.

"Oh. Quinn…yes!"

Quinn glanced up to see her going wild. She was rocking against his fingers, helping him as he slid them in and out of her. She was ready, so he took her clit in his mouth and sucked on it, all the while flicking it with his tongue.

"Ohhh…oh…Quinn…oooh." Ann's muscles contracted and sent a vibrating sensation to course through every part of her body as she flew.

Quinn felt her orgasm as it tore through her body. He felt the reverberation against his fingers which were still deep inside her. The rush of fluid that came from her was exquisite. It was the sweetest most overwhelming thing he had ever experienced.

He had tasted her before when she came, but it seemed different now, hotter, and so rich. It was like the sweetest nectar. He lapped it up and gloried in the fact was he had given her that. He was drinking from her the passion which he had created. *God, he loved her.*

Ann came in a surging heat of passion. Hot, white lightning coursed through her body as his fingers stayed inside her ass. Her juices flowed as Quinn continued to use his mouth on her quivering flesh. As much as she wanted to enjoy the pleasure his mouth was giving her, she needed more. Despite his fingers, she still felt so empty.

"Quinn, I want more."

Quinn looked up at her, amused at her brazenness. Normally when it came to sex talk, she could be so shy. But now her demands were sexy as hell. "What do you want ,baby?"

Ann looked over at the items she purchased. Hoping that he would understand, without her having to tell him.

"Do you want to try the plug honey?" He waited for her answer as he gently slid his fingers from her.

"Yesss..." She moaned her answer, wishing he hadn't have removed his fingers.

Quinn walked over to the other side of the bed and removed the butt plug from its packaging. He then studied the three lubricants that she bought. There was grape, watermelon and cherry. He grinned, definitely cherry. Opening the seal to the bottle he turned to her.

"Get up honey. I'll be right there."

Quinn walked over to her with the butt plug in one hand and the lubricant in the other. He held the plug out to her. "Do you want to see it before we get started?"

Ann grabbed the phallic-shaped toy. It had a flat end on it and a tiny button on that same end. "What's this for?"

He smiled at her as he reached down and hit the button. "For this?"

Ann almost jumped clear out of her skin. It vibrates? She didn't know that. What's more, it sounded like heaven. *What would it feel like? Oh God.* She couldn't wait anymore. She handed it back to him, "I'm ready."

Quinn set the items on the bed and pulled his briefs down. He wasn't able to hide his delight at the hunger that washed over her face when she saw him spring out of his shorts. He lay down on the bed and propped his head up on the pillows. "Come here." He motioned for her to get on top of him.

Ann didn't understand how he was going to do this if she was, oh— "Did you mean face the other way?"

He smiled at her. "Yeah, honey. I want to see every inch of your tight ass when I do this to you for the first time."

Chapter Seventeen

For the first time? Oh God. Could someone actually come from words alone? Because she was damn close. She turned around and was met with the sight of his magnificent cock. She didn't wait for permission. She bent her head and took him deep into her mouth. She loved the smoothness of his skin when he was so hard. It was such an erotic contradiction. A large, hard cock with smooth, velvety soft skin that tasted so good.

Quinn had to reign in his control. When he felt her mouth take him in he wanted to start pumping into her with everything that he had. But he knew he had to wait. He reached over and grabbed the pink toy and the bottom of lubrication. He flipped the cap up, squirted some to the very tip and watched as it drizzled down the sides. As he flipped the cap closed, he bit back a curse that wanted to tear from his lips when she licked the underside of his cock.

Ann loved this. She loved teasing him, tasting him, loving him and fucking him with her mouth. How on earth she ever could have thought he was too big was amazing to her. He was complete perfection.

Quinn rubbed lube all over the butt plug, making sure that every inch of it was covered in cherry-smelling slickness. "I'm gonna start honey. Are you ready?"

She moaned her reply and scooted herself further to him. Had she ever wanted anything so badly in her entire life? She felt completely hollow inside. The overwhelming feeling of needing to be filled so completely was only intensifying.

Quinn slid the toy into the seam of her ass and placed the tip at her entrance. The sight of her tiny puckered hole was exquisite. He wanted to give her this, to show her how much pleasure she could have, but he was barely holding onto the last amount of restraint he had left. He couldn't wait until he was able to take her there. To fill her so completely with himself.

Ann felt the pressure of the tip as Quinn held it against her opening. "Quinn, please. I need to feel it." She no longer cared how desperate she sounded. She wanted to feel that funny-shaped toy inside of her; she wanted him to turn it on as it vibrated inside of her in a place that had never known any intrusion before Quinn.

Quinn heard the desperation in her voice and didn't wait for her to ask him a second time. Gently and slowly he barely slid the tip inside. He heard her moan as she rocked further against him, causing it to slide in a little further.

"Are you okay, honey?" He had to know. He didn't want to hurt her.

"No, Quinn I need more." She was beyond pleading, beyond urgent. She was demanding now.

Quinn listened to the ardent tone of her voice in disbelief. He applied a little more pressure and intended to be slow in his intimate trespass of her virginal hole, but she didn't let him. He was stunned when she eased back further into it and slid it completely inside of her. Granted it was only five inches long but with its odd bowling pin shape it was as big as an inch in diameter in some points. He never thought she would accept it so willingly. But she did and she was moaning in pleasure from it. Quinn took the hint and hit the little button at the end of the flat surface, turning on the vibration.

Ann jolted. *Oh…my…*"Quinn…it's…oh God…" What was happening to her? She couldn't even take him in her mouth she was so distracted from the sensations flowing through her body.

"Does it feel good, honey?" Quinn knew it did, but the alpha male in him needed to hear how much she loved it.

“Oh yes…Quinn…it’s…so…oh God…Quinn…I’m gonna…I can’t take it much long…oooh.” Ann didn’t know how, but within sixty seconds of that tiny toy being pushed inside and the vibration hitting every sensitive wall inside of her, she came.

Quinn was in awe. He listened and watched her body buck with pleasure as she came, causing her sweetness to pour out of her onto his chest. He was dying for her. Whenever he thought, there was no way that he could possibly want her more she found new ways to drive him insane with lust for her.

“Oh damn, babe. That was amazing.” He told her as he aggressively massaged the globes of her ass. Dying to plunge into her and take her.

She had to laugh. “You think that was amazing. Just imagine what it felt like, it was so incredible.” She told him as she leered over her shoulder at him. Feeling flirty, she said, “Do you have more for me?”

Quinn saw the blush on her face, which he knew was from part arousal, part uncertainty. She was trying so hard to seduce him with her words that he had to smile. What she didn’t realize was that just looking at her was all the seduction he needed.

“You want more, baby? Tell me what you want. Tell me what you want me to do to you.” He needed her to open up to him completely. He wanted her to be that brazen woman on the side of the road that had begged him to fuck her.

“Quinn please.” She hated that she could get so embarrassed by the thoughts that went through her head. “I need you. All of you, inside of me…there.”

No freaking way was he going to wait any longer. “Get up, honey.”

He watched as she scooted forward. The plug was still inside of her, vibrating and with every move she made she whimpered. Once she was completely off of him he got up from the bed. He reached for the cherry lubricant and liberally applied some to his engorged cock. If he wasn’t careful he thought he was going to lose it right then.

Quinn got on the bed behind her. "Turn just a little, babe. I want you to face the mirror. I need to see you when I take you here."

She did as he asked and moved just a bit to her left. She looked up and saw him in the mirror's reflection. She was on all fours and he was looming behind her. Her whole body was humming with pleasure from the plug which was still assaulting her ass in the best possible way.

Quinn reached down and pulled the pink toy from her and shut it off. He had to laugh when she muffled a protest. "It's okay, honey. Just hang on."

He looked down at her glistening hole. The lubrication had left a shiny coating along the outside of it and it was gaping open just a tiny bit from the little invasion that the plug had given her. He was suddenly worried. He looked at the tiny, tight little opening and glanced at his erection. *How on earth was she going to be able to take him?*

"Ann...honey, are you sure?"

She looked at him in the mirror. "Yes. Quinn, I love you. I trust you."

He loved her too, so much, which is why he was hesitating. "It's going to hurt, baby. Do you understand that? It's going to hurt really bad at first."

She swallowed, trying to keep her nerves at bay. "Don't you want to?"

"Of course I do." He slid his fingers inside of her and played them around, massaging the inner walls as she moaned and moved against him. "I want it more than you know. But I need you to understand that it might really hurt you."

Ann bit down on her bottom lip, torn between the wonderful feeling of his fingers and the nerves that were clawing at her. "Will it hurt...a lot? I mean, I know it will, but will it get better?"

Quinn dropped his head and placed a light kiss to one of her cheeks. "Yeah, honey. It will get a lot better. I promise that no matter how much it hurts, that I will make it good for you in the end." He looked back up at her. "Do you trust me to do that for you?"

She nodded. "Yes. I trust you. Show me how it can feel, Quinn. Take me where no man ever has."

"Okay honey. I'm gonna go slow, okay? Just try and relax. If you tense up it will hurt more, so just relax. Think about how good it's going to feel." Quinn slid his fingers from her and fisted his cock in his hand.

Ann waited; her pulse was pounding so fast she thought her heart might leap clear out of her chest. Then she felt it. He was nudging her entrance. This was it. Do or die time. She prayed that she would have the strength and the will power to handle the pain and discomfort, because she wanted this. She needed to feel all of him deep inside of her.

Quinn entered her with the head of his penis. He hesitated and watched her in the mirror when he heard her gasp in pain. He knew how hard this must be for her. Even the biggest part of the butt plug wasn't as big as he was. No matter how much they had played, her body wasn't ready to accept the size of him. He pulled back and out of her.

"I'm sorry, honey."

"Quinn, why did you stop?"

"Baby, I was hurting you." He ran a hand underneath her to massage a nipple, needing to feel the erect little points.

"No. I mean yes, it hurt, but I kind of liked it. I need you, I want this, please, Quinn." She wouldn't allow him to stop now, not when they were so close to what they both wanted.

"You're absolutely sure? Because if you want me to stop, just tell me, honey. Can you promise me that?" He needed to be sure that she knew that she came first, above all else.

Now she was getting irritated. She was aching for him to take her there. "Yes, damn it, Quinn. I need you to fuck me. Just do it. I'm dying to feel all of you."

Quinn was shocked by her demanding tone. He grinned at her, "Yes ma'am."

He fisted his cock once more, taking a deep breath he reigned in his control to keep from losing it right then. He positioned himself at her slick, puckered entrance. Knowing that he was hard enough and there was enough lubrication, he didn't need to guide himself. Instead, he took his hands and spread her cheeks apart. He groaned and slid the head inside. *Fuck!* He had slid in further this time and she was tighter than he had ever thought imaginable.

Ann felt him go deeper and it did hurt, but it was a good hurt. If there was such a thing. Because despite the pain, she felt so incredibly happy. She wondered why he had stopped and looked up at him in the mirror. "What's wrong?" She asked him.

Quinn had to laugh. "Honey, if I move right now, I'm gonna come. Just give me a second okay?"

She smiled at him, loving the fact that he was just as turned on as she was. But the truth of it was that it made her feel kind of powerful. She wasn't ashamed to admit she liked that feeling of power either. She took a deep breath and relaxed every muscle in her body. She could feel her muscles throbbing with the intrusion of his large cock in such a tiny hole. But she didn't care, she wanted, needed more of him. Ann slid back just a bit as she watched him grit his teeth.

Quinn watched her as she slid further onto his cock. "Oh Annie. Fuck you feel so good." At this point he didn't care if he came or not, because all that mattered was giving her what she wanted. What they both wanted.

"I'm gonna go all the way, babe. Are you ready?"

Was she ever. The pain was subsiding and now she just felt tiny little sensations shooting from her sensitive inner muscles straight to her pussy. As wet as she was earlier, she knew that she was dripping right now. "Yes Quinn, I want all of you."

Quinn grabbed her hips and took a moment to look her in the eyes before he completed the connection between their bodies. "I love you,

Annie." And without waiting for a response he slid into her all the way.

Ann shot up from her position. She was no longer leaning over on her hands, but sitting up on her knees, Quinn's arms wrapped around her as she clung to him. He was completely and totally inside of her. She could feel his balls brushing against her pussy. *This was it, heaven.* He was giving her such a complete feeling of fullness. Without her knowledge, a tear escaped one of her eyes as she stared at his reflection.

Quinn was shocked. She hadn't pulled away, but had welcomed him into her. But there was a tear trailing down her cheek. "Oh babe. Did I hurt you?"

She shook her head. "No, no you've made me so happy. Quinn, I love you so much. This feels so incredible."

How did she always manage to find a way to make him love her more? "It feels amazing, honey. Will you do me a favor?"

She turned her head and kissed the side of his neck. "Anything. I'll do anything for you, Quinn."

"Get back down on your hands, honey. I want to see your ass as I fuck you there. I want to watch while I pump in and out of your tiny hole." Quinn loved what his words did to her. He saw the desire wash over her.

She was dying for him. She wanted this, him, everything. So she did as he asked her to. She released him from her grasp and slid back down while he was still inside of her. Relishing in the fullness that she felt from him being so deep inside of her.

Quinn massaged her cheeks and spread them further apart. He looked at the pink puckered ring of skin surrounding his cock and started to slide back and forth in her. *Oh yeah, she felt so tight, so good.* He remembered something else she had bought. Not wanting to stop what he was doing, he grabbed onto the bedspread and tugged it until the tiny fingertip vibrator slid closer within his reach.

Ann watched him in the mirror. She knew what he was going to do, and she loved him for it. As good as it felt to be filled by him she knew the sensation of that tiny vibrator against her clit would surely make her come again.

Quinn grabbed the tiny box that held the toy and ripped it open, throwing the packaging across the room. "Put this on your finger, Annie. I want you to use it on yourself."

She was surprised by his request. When she bought it, she assumed he would use it on her. But she reached her hand back and took it from him. She slid it on the forefinger of her right hand and reached her hand up at Quinn.

"How does it turn on?"

Quinn reached over her, barely holding on as he continued to glide his cock in and out of her ass. He pressed the tiny button at the base of it and laughed when she jumped at the feeling. "Use it, honey. Pleasure yourself. Let me watch you make yourself come."

Ann reached her hand down and was about to touch herself with it when she stopped. She looked up at Quinn and smiled at him, "I love you, Quinn. I don't need this, you know. This feels so good. I want you to know that. I want you to know how good you feel deep inside of me."

Oh, honey. "Then show me, Annie. Rub your clit with that little toy you bought, because when you do I am gonna fuck you hard."

Something about the way his voice changed made her even hotter for him. She reached her hand down and touched the tiny vibrating head to her sensitive and swollen nub. *Oh Jesus!*

Quinn started thrusting into her harder and faster than he ever thought he would be able to in such a tiny hole. But he watched her face and he knew how much she loved it. Words couldn't describe the feelings that were consuming him. He was already so close.

"Quinn…oh…it's…yes…harder…oh God…faster…Quinn…I'm gonna come…"

Quinn went from staring at her tight hole as he invaded it with every thrust to staring at her reflection in the mirror. She met his every demand as he plunged into her. She was fucking him just as hard as he was fucking her. It was incredible.

"Annie, you feel so good baby. You're so tight. I love you so much." Quinn was thrusting into her with zeal. Taking her like a madman. "I can't last much longer. I have to come, honey. Come with me."

She was already there. She ground the tiny vibrator against her clit one last time and exploded over her hand. She was so overwhelmed with the ecstasy enveloping her entire body that she couldn't speak, she merely gasped in pleasure as her body bucked with the orgasm.

Quinn felt it. Felt her muscles contract and pulse against the walls of her ass. It was different from when she came when he was inside of her pussy. Instead of milking and coaxing him, this was like a velvet jackhammer beating against his cock until he spurt with his release.

"Fuck baby, yes!" Quinn let go of the demon clawing at the base of his spine kick him over the edge into oblivion. He came inside of her and felt his hot fluid wash back over him in the tight opening. Jesus. Unable to control himself, he thrust inside of her several more times to complete the euphoric agony that was continuing to claw at his very soul.

They watched each other in the mirror, amazed at one another and what they had just experienced. Quinn was the first to regain his composure and smiled at her. He needed to hold her, to be closer to her. He slid out and pulled her up to him. He wrapped his arms around her and held her body tightly to his chest.

Ann's heart was in her throat. This was it, the final connection. He hadn't just fucked her in her ass. He had taken possession of her, penetrated her very soul by the act. They truly belonged to one another now. She turned to face him, needing to feel his warm breath as it washed across her face.

Quinn looked into her eyes and saw the tiny glistening tears. "Honey, are you okay?"

She nodded and blinked, causing the tears to slide down her cheeks. "I'm so happy, Quinn. I love you so much. And you were right." She kissed him before continuing. "That was amazing. I've never felt so close to you. I belong to you. I hope you know that. I hope you know that I trust you completely. There is nothing I wouldn't let you do to me, with me."

Quinn grinned, "Is my shy little Annie becoming more brazen?"

She nodded and blushed. "It's all your fault. You bring out the naughty little woman in me."

Quinn held her closer and whispered into her ear. "Well, in that case. I bet there is a whole section in that store that we could get lost in."

Ann laughed before looking up at him. "There actually were a few things that looked sort of…interesting."

"Yeah, we'll have to check it out sometime. Now come here. I'm going to run you a hot bath." Quinn pulled her off of the bed and onto her feet. "Then, we will have the rest of our lives together to experiment."

"Quinn." She nudged him playfully and giggled, but was secretly anticipating what new things they could try.

"I love you, honey. We're going to have a great life together." He was brushing his hands up and down her arms. Still not able to believe his luck.

Ann fluttered her eyelashes up at him. "You know that fantasy list I was telling you about?"

He nodded. "Mmm hmm."

She looked over at the cowboy hat hanging on the hook behind the door. "Well, there's nothing hotter than a man in a cowboy hat."

He laughed. "What are you saying? Ride 'em cowboy?"

This time she nodded. "Yeah, maybe. Come on cowboy, take a bath with me." And she walked towards the bathroom.

"Honey if I get in that bath with you, you know what's going to happen." He warned her.

She turned back to look at him over her shoulder. "I was sort of counting on it." She reached up, grabbed the Stetson and sashayed into the bathroom.

Quinn listened to the water start and walked towards the bathroom. *Hell. He was one lucky son of a bitch!*

Epilogue

Derek's Story Begins...

Derek rested his head back against the seat of the cab. His flight had been long, too long. And he was completely exhausted. All he wanted to do was find a bed and sleep. But unfortunately he knew that Zach was waiting for him. He still couldn't believe he was going where he was going. Zach, an old buddy of his from high school had always been a bit on the daring side. However Derek never imagined in his wildest dreams that he was into the BDSM scene. What was even more shocking was Derek's quick reply to Zach's invitation. He jumped at the chance.

So after Quinn and Ann had gotten back from their honeymoon, which had been a hellacious two weeks of running between the Roadhouse and the restaurant constantly trying to keep everything on an even keel, he told the newlyweds that he was in desperate need of a vacation.

Of course they had been gracious, told him to leave and take as long as he needed. Which was easy for them to say, he thought. Because they were two people, it would be a piece of cake for them to watch the two businesses. He had to laugh. Actually, they were two halves of the same person. In the past six months, leading up to their wedding they had literally turned into one another. They finished each other's sentences and did things for one another without the other person even needing to ask. Although Derek couldn't be one hundred percent positive, he was pretty sure that they mated like the damn energizer bunny on a double shot espresso.

"We're here, sir." The grungy cab driver said from the front seat.

Derek glanced at the red numbers which displayed his fare amount. He reached into his pocket for a twenty dollar bill and handed it to the man. "Here, keep the change."

After Derek got his luggage out of the trunk, the cab drove away, taking the stench with it. *Thank God.*

So here it was. Wow. Apparently the BDSM scene was moving up in the world. The few clubs that Derek had been to several years ago had always been 'underground' establishments. They were either in old warehouses or run down lofts, but never had Derek been to one that looked like this. He stood there studying it for a moment when the large double doors opened.

Zach opened the front doors and walked out to greet Derek. Once he got to the bottom of the long front walkway he held out his hand.

"Welcome to Pleasure Seekers, old friend."

"Old friend? We're not sixty Zach." But Derek held his hand out to him. "It's good to see you. I see the military kept you in shape."

Zach laughed. "Yes, well I see that you are still blessed with the natural physique of an athlete. But if memory serves, you do nothing to earn it. You still as lazy as you always were?"

Derek shrugged. "Not when it matters."

Zach only nodded his agreement. "Come. Let me show you to your room. I think you'll like it."

Twenty minutes later Derek was turning on the shower to try to wash off his jet lag. He knew he had to hurry. Zach had told him one of the newest members was having problems adjusting to her role as a submissive. For whatever reason Zach had thought that Derek would be the perfect Dom to teach her.

Derek felt a little, no, a lot uneasy that Zach knew so much about Derek's preferable role in the BDSM world. Just from a few of the comments that Zach had made, Derek would have sworn that their paths might have crossed at one of those clubs he'd attended in the past. But for the life of him he couldn't remember seeing Zach since high school.

Quickly, Derek washed his body and jumped out of the shower. He had only minutes to get his game face on and meet Zach in what he called, 'The Learning Room.' Seven years ago he wouldn't have needed to prepare himself, for what he was about to do. But seven years ago he hadn't met Sandi. It was approaching the two year mark since their break up and Derek still hadn't managed to sleep with another woman.

He laughed as he yanked up his leather pants. It was actually kind of pathetic. Here he was a Dom, not by practice or frequency, but by nature, and he hadn't even fucked a woman in almost two years.

Derek ran a hand through his still damp hair and headed towards The Learning Room. He knocked once and waited for someone to say it was all right to enter. When Zach gave him permission he came in.

"Derek, this young woman you see tied to the bed is the one I was telling you about. She is having trouble adjusting." Zach shrugged as he walked towards the door. "See, it's complicated. As much as she craves this lifestyle, she wants to be controlled, to the extent of punishment."

Derek was about to tell Zach that wasn't that unusual, he had dealt with many subs who held the same desires. But Zach quickly interrupted him.

"No, I see what you're thinking and you misunderstand. She is not in it for the pleasure. She doesn't want to feel good, only pain. That is where you come in. If she is serious about becoming a member, she either has to learn to enjoy the pleasure that the pain can bring or she will have to leave."

Derek listened to Zach's explanation, which basically meant that this sub sought no sexual release. Even with the different levels of Doms and subs there was always an eventual release. No matter how rough things got, it was for the purpose of the ultimate pleasure. But, according to Zach she only wanted pain.

"You see," Zach continued as reached to open the door. "She feels guilty about something in her past. She believes that if she continues to take the pain and humiliation, that it will somehow make up for what she did. Do you understand?"

Derek nodded as he motioned for Zach to leave them alone. Once the door was finally shut Derek walked over to the table that held an assortment of pleasure props. He fingered a couple of them before deciding on a crop. He walked behind the woman. She was on all fours, her hands tied to the headboard in front of her. Her head was facing the wall as her ass was jutting upward.

Smack! Derek didn't want to give her time to anticipate. He only wanted her to feel. *Smack, smack!* He slapped her again and again with the jockey's instrument, only harder this time. His eyes glinted in satisfaction at the red welts forming on her rear.

She looked magnificent. Beautiful pale white skin, marred by redness of his doing. His cock hardened. He had missed this. *The control. The lust. The power.*

Derek wanted to feel her, and his job as her Dom was to teach her to enjoy it. How would she be able to deny pleasure if he was fucking her? If there was one thing Derek was confident of, it was his ability to fuck a woman senseless.

He pulled the snap free on his pants and peeled away the front opening. These pants had been made especially for this kind of easy access. He walked over to the table and picked up a condom. He sheathed himself and got on the bed behind her.

She was still so quiet. She hadn't moved or said anything, not even made a noise since he'd walked in. He was going to change that. His first rule when he was trying to train a submissive was to teach her the earth-shattering pleasure part of it first. Then when they were dying with need for it, there was nothing they wouldn't submit to. They would belong to the Dom, willing to do anything to make them happy.

Now at her entrance he weighed his options, he could coax her, but he wanted her to suffer just a little, to remember who was in charge. Instead, he placed his hands on her ass cheeks and pulled them far apart, effectively giving him access to her wet—yep, that's right, she was wet—pussy.

Derek laughed. *So she didn't want pleasure from it, huh? Then why was she dripping with need?* Derek stared at her opening for a moment. A strange feeling overcame him. He couldn't place it, so he ignored it. And with a swift thrust, he was deep inside her.

Jesus! She was clinging to him, massaging his cock as her pussy trembled around him. Maybe it had been because he hadn't had sex in so long, or maybe it was because she was so tight, but he was in heaven at the feel of her wet heat enveloping him.

Derek was ready to fuck her with an intensity that he hadn't known in a very long time when that feeling washed back over him. She felt so*...oh shit!*

"Sandi?" He asked the one word question, praying he was wrong.

The once quiet and motionless woman swung her head around to face him. Horrified, she looked at him. "Derek?"

THE END

www.nicolemorgan1.webs.com

ABOUT THE AUTHOR

Nicole Morgan is an avid reader who kept having one recurring problem. Ideas of stories kept popping into her head. She ignored her desire to write until her curiosity got the better of her and she decided to research what steps she would have to take if she truly wanted to take a chance and write.

Nicole took a chance and followed her dream. She has been blessed with some fabulous opportunities and has met some wonderful people along the way. Writing is a true love to her and has brought her a new and profound happiness with every step she's taken along the way.

Siren Publishing, Inc.
www.SirenPublishing.com

LaVergne, TN USA
20 May 2010
183246LV00006B/74/P

9 781606 015995